PARISIAN STORIES

Parisian Stories

HAMON DE QUILLAN

Contents

PART ONE

The Girl With the Red Hair

Chapter 1

An Unusual Encounter in Paris

In the heart of Paris, a bustling café buzzed with the sounds of laughter and clinking cups. Amidst the horde of patrons, Leila sat alone at a small round table, her striking red hair a vibrant flame against the muted tones of the café. She immersed herself in a book, yet her aura radiated an unspoken charm that danced in the air around her. It was then that Mahmoud entered, his presence commanding attention as he navigated through the throng of people. When his eyes met hers, the world fell away, leaving only the two of them in that brief, electric moment. Something deeper ignited within him as he felt an unusual connection; a blend of familiarity and fascination that sent shivers down his spine.

As he approached her, she looked up, and a smile flitted across her lips, soft yet full of mystery. Do you always read in crowded places? he asked, his voice barely louder than the hum of conversation. Only when the world outside feels too quiet, she replied, her eyes glinting with mischief. They exchanged a few more words, each syllable dripping with a sweetness that lingered long after. Mahmoud's heart raced as he parted ways, each step away from her shrouded in a veil of longing. The brief encounter left him with an unsettling sense of déjà vu, a feeling as if he had known her in another life, in a realm untouched by the passing of time.

* * *

Leila's vibrant hair seems part of her spirit and individuality, drawing the eyes of everyone who crossed her path. In the bustling streets of Paris, where the echoes of history mingled with the whispers of modern romance, her fiery mane swayed like a flame dancing in the wind. The city that cradled her dreams and ambitions became a tapestry upon which her boldness painted its strokes. Students would steal glances during Professor Mahmoud's lectures, their attention momentarily captured by the allure of her red locks, an emblem of her nonconformity and innocence intertwined.

Mahmoud, a seasoned professor of Arab literature, often found himself lost in reflections as Leila spoke about her passion for poetry. The sound of her voice wrapped in the color red resonated deeply within him, reminding him of the profound beauty that lay within this particular hue. Red was not merely a color; it was an embodiment of passion, love, and all-consuming desire. As he leaned against the weathered oak of the classroom lectern, he could not help but think of the way red ignited emotions long buried in heart and soul. You know, Leila, he would muse, red captivates and confounds. It is, after all, the color of the heart's deepest yearnings.

During their shared moments, Mahmoud began to see that the charisma of Leila extended beyond her hair; it was as if the very essence of her being vibrated with an alluring mystery. The pauses in conversation lingered in the air, thick with tension and unspoken words, drawing them ever closer together. In the enchanting evenings of Paris, beneath the glow of street-lamps, their laughter echoed like music, a symphony only they could hear. Their journey would unfold across cities; the bustling markets of Tunis, the quiet cafés in London, and the sun-soaked streets of Cairo, where shared moments would blossom into something undeniable. There was a destiny in motion, guided by the elegance of red, the color that whispered of love waiting to be released. Whoever embraces life with passion, like Leila's radiant hair, weaves a story etched deeper and more beautifully than mere words can convey.

* * *

Her striking red hair glowed like embers in the Paris sun, drawing the eyes of passersby and igniting a warmth in the otherwise brisk air of the university courtyard. She walked with a delicate grace, her movements reminiscent of a dancer gliding through an unseen rhythm. Each day in class, Mahmoud found himself entranced not just by her beauty but by the way her mind worked, blooming with thoughts unlike anything he had encountered in years. It was in the way she interpreted classic texts, weaving intricate narratives that seemed to hold secrets of their own. The occasional exchange of glances between them felt electric, a charge that hummed in the space around them. He would often catch her smiling softly at his lectures, her gaze piercing into the depths of his soul, igniting a fire of intrigue.

A lingering question stirred within him: Is there more to Leila than meets the eye? Every conversation with her unfolded layers, revealing glimpses of a history wrapped in complexity. She spoke of her Tunisian roots with a longing in her voice, hinting at stories filled with untold hardships and vibrant tales of resilience. When she would laugh, it bubbled forth with a melody that hinted at joyous secrets, dancing within the echoes of her words. Mahmoud sensed a duality within her; one moment, she was the spirited student eager for knowledge, and the next, a shadow of something deeper lurked behind her laughter. As he pondered this, each literature seminar turned into a quest, one that filled his heart with longing and his mind with questions. They began discussing poetry in their evening classes, and with every verse she uttered, Mahmoud felt a deep-rooted yearning to unravel the enigma that was Leila, and perhaps, to discover if she could be the muse that had been absent from his life for too long.

Days turned into weeks, and their intellectual exchanges often transcended the classroom walls, spilling into quiet cafes where the aroma of espresso intertwined with whispered aspirations. Each conversation beckoned a dance of words, leaving Mahmoud captivated. He could no longer separate his fascination for literature from the feelings stirring in his heart. One rainy afternoon, while sharing an umbrella, their laughter mingled with the sound of falling drops, creating a symphony that seemed only for them.

"What is it that you see in the texts we read, Mahmoud?" Leila asked, her eyes searching his with a gentle intensity.

His breath caught for a moment as he realized she could sense the pull between them too, an unspoken bond tethered by curiosity and longing.

"I see our stories within them," he replied, feeling the weight of truth in his words.

In that moment, under the drizzling Parisian sky, they shared a secret spark, igniting a flame of possibility, a whispered promise of exploration yet to come.

Chapter 2

Whispers of Literature

The walls, adorned with faded maps of the Middle East, resonate with the whispers of ancient verses. Sunlight streams through tall windows, illuminating the dust motes that dance like the spirits of poets long past. Each word Mahmoud speaks takes flight, weaving through the air with the elegance of a gazelle. His voice, rich and warm, invites his students into the depths of a world where every syllable carries the weight of history, the breath of longing, and the pulse of love.

At the front of the room, Leila sits with her fiery red hair cascading over her shoulders, caught in the magnetic pull of his eloquence. To her, Mahmoud is not just a professor; he is an embodiment of every romantic tale her heart yearns to explore. The way his eyebrows dance when he delves into the verses of Al-Mutanabbi or the way his eyes light up when he recounts the love stories woven through Arab literature fills her with an intoxicating thrill. Each glance exchanged is electric, tinged with an unspoken possibility. Her heart races, its rhythm echoing the stanzas he recites.

"What a perfect metaphor for the heart," she muses silently, feeling as if they are the only ones in the room.

As he closes a book of poetry, Mahmoud pauses and locks eyes with Leila, his gaze lingering for a heartbeat longer. She lets out a soft breath, her pulse quickening at the weight of the moment. The classroom fades away, leaving just the two of them swirling in a world filled with unexpressed words.

"What do you think, Leila? Can love be as fleeting as a poem yet as enduring as the stars?" he asks, his voice low, a smile playing at the corners of his mouth.

Her response is a soft whisper:

"Love is eternal; it lives in every line, every heartbeat."

The air crackles with the tension of unspoken desires and lingering questions, propelling the quiet romance of student and teacher toward an unknown destination filled with adventure that stretches from the boulevards of Paris to the bustling streets of Cairo. Embracing the path of an enduring love story, Leila feels an irresistible pull toward Mahmoud, the enigmatic professor who has awakened her soul.

* * *

Mahmoud stood in front of the classroom, his gaze drifting across the faces of his students. The air was heavy with anticipation, filled with the scent of aging books and freshly brewed coffee. With a gentle rhythm, he recited a forgotten poem, the words steeped in a nostalgia that seemed to awaken something deep within Leila.

A delicate hush fell over the room as his voice danced through verses rich with longing and loss. The vibrant echoes of his articulation shimmered like stars in a clear Tunisian night, igniting a fire in her heart. Each line he spoke painted a landscape of beautiful despair, and she could feel the past ripple through her veins, drawing her closer to the essence of Mahmoud's world.

* * *

In the lecture hall of the Sorbonne, where the air was thick with the fragrance of old books and whispered dreams, Leila's gaze drifted across the rows of students. It was there, amidst the quiet murmur of anticipation, that her eyes met Mahmoud's, the celebrated professor of Arab literature. His dark, thoughtful eyes held an intensity that sent a shiver through her spine, awakening a longing she had yet to understand.

The world around them faded, leaving only the weight of unspoken desires hanging in the air, a fleeting connection that felt both exhilarating and terrifying. There was familiarity in that glance, as if they were two characters lost in a story waiting to be written, filled with nuances of fate and chance.

In that electric moment, time seemed to suspend itself, as if the universe conspired to reveal a truth hidden beneath the surface of their lives. Mahmoud, always the composed scholar, found himself vulnerable, caught off-guard by the spark ignited by Leila's fiery red hair; a blaze of passion among the muted tones of the classroom. He noticed how she bit her lip in concentration, the delicate curve betraying a whirlwind of thoughts, perhaps of poetry or the intricate tales they dissected. She was an enigma, and yet her presence stirred a familiar hope within him, a sense that perhaps they shared a secret that transcended the boundaries of age and authority.

As the class unfolded around them, each word from the professor's lips danced on the cusp of significance, layering their moment with meaning. The tension hung between them like a delicate thread, ready to snap with even the slightest touch. After the lecture, their paths crossed again in the bustling corridors of the university, filled with the voices of students sharing dreams and aspirations.

"I found your thoughts on 'One Thousand and One Nights' quite compelling, Professor," Leila ventured, her cheeks flushed, not just from the warmth of the room but from the weight of their shared glance.

Mahmoud turned to her, a smile flickering across his face:

"And I found your interpretation refreshing, Leila. Tell me more."

Both felt the thrill of possibilities ahead, their hearts racing as the world beyond blended into the backdrop of a blooming connection.

Chapter 3

The Veil of Secrets

Leila was a girl with a heart full of curiosity, her vibrant red hair a banner of her fiery spirit. Though she had grown up in Paris, her mind often wandered to far-off places, especially to Tunisia, her father's homeland. She had heard stories of its sun-drenched streets and the rich aroma of spices lingering in the air. The tales her father told were like threads woven into the fabric of her identity, yet they felt distant and fragmented, like a half-remembered dream. Intrigued by her roots, she purchased a ticket to Tunis, her anticipation mingling with the scent of jasmine that hung in the Parisian air as she prepared for her journey. Every heartbeat seemed to echo with the rhythm of history waiting to be uncovered.

Walking the bustling streets of the Medina, Leila felt as if the stones whispered stories of her ancestors. Every narrow alleyway seemed to lead her deeper into a world that teemed with life and color. She paused outside a café, where the laughter of patrons floated through the air like a warm breeze. As she took a seat, the muted hues of orange and lavender danced in the sun, pushing away the remnants of unfamiliarity. Each sip of mint tea tasted of nostalgia. In the laughter of the people and the majestic archways, she began to see pieces of herself reflected back. It was here that she stumbled upon a worn-out bookshop nestled between vibrant stalls, a hidden gem brimming with forgotten stories that seemed to beckon her forward. This was the start of her journey; a journey that would connect her not only to her heritage but to the fragmented past of a man named Mahmoud.

Mahmoud, a professor of Arab literature at the Sorbonne, named Leila's tutor and guide through the intricate weave of Arabic poetry and prose. He had his own ties to Tunisia, and with each lesson, he introduced her to a world where words painted the sunsets and silenced the storms. As they navigated the landscapes of historic texts, Leila noticed how every poem whispered Mahmoud's own history; a tale of loss, love, and rediscovery. Together they explored each corner of the citadel, their fingers tracing the rough stone as they spoke of lost cities and buried dreams. In their shared laughter and fleeting glances, an unspoken bond grew, feeding the flames of their respective journeys. Life, they learned, was much like the tales of old: woven with strands of love, loss, and hope, always leading back home. The roads ahead were uncertain, yet together they ventured into the heart of Tunis, ready to unveil secrets of time that would intertwine their fates forever.

* * *

In a bustling market in the heart of Paris, Leila wandered among the stalls, each brimming with treasures of the mind and spirit. She spotted a peculiar book tucked between the cracked covers of forgotten novels. Its spine was worn, and the faded lettering whispered promises of poetry that spoke of love and longing. With a sense of destiny, she pulled the book from the shelf and felt an inexplicable connection to its pages. Inside, she discovered verses that echoed the scholarly work of Mahmoud, her professor. The rhythms of his lectures danced in her mind, intertwining with the lyrical prose of long-lost poets. Each line seemed to bridge the gap between their worlds, blending the passions of the past with the undeniable chemistry resounding in the present.

The vibrant chaos of the market mirrored the complexities of her feelings for Mahmoud. Colorful stalls burst with life, aromas of spices perfuming the air as vendors called out their wares. Leila felt caught in the whirlwind of colors and sounds, much like the whirlwind of emotions that surging within her. She remembered their encounters at the Sorbonne, late-night discussions and stolen glances, where the subtleties of language transformed into something more profound. With each heartbeat, the thrumming pulse of the market compelled her to acknowledge her affection, a silent yet powerful force binding them together, deepening their connection. She could almost hear the echo of his voice weaving through the crowded space, imploring her to embrace the beauty of her own story, even if it seemed lost among the myriad of voices surrounding her. Just as she closed the book, a soft touch grazed her arm; an instant that held the promise of fate.

** * **

In the heart of Tunis, amidst the ancient streets that whispered secrets of bygone eras, fate orchestrated a serendipitous encounter. Leila, with her fiery red hair dancing in the breeze, strolled through the bustling market, a vibrant tapestry of colors and fragrances enveloping her. The air was rich with the scent of spices, as vendors called out, their voices blending into a melodic cacophony. Just then, Mahmoud emerged from a narrow alley, his expression contemplative, a book clutched in one hand. Their eyes met, and in that fleeting second, the world around them faded into silence. Both felt an electric charge, as if the universe conspired to bring together this unexpected pairing.

"Leila," he murmured, his voice a soft invitation that lingered in the air. "You look as if you've stepped out of a story."

As they wandered through the stalls, sharing fragments of their lives, the connection deepened, transforming into a bridge spanning dreams and desires. Each word they exchanged unfolded layers of unspoken longing, as Leila spoke of Parisian nights filled with possibilities, while Mahmoud reflected on the tales steeped in the sands of time. That chance meeting, under the warm Tunisian sun, cemented an invisible bond; two souls navigating their personal labyrinths suddenly entwined.

"I've always believed," Mahmoud said, a hint of seriousness in his eyes, "that love finds us when we least expect it."

Leila nodded, feeling his words wrap around her like a soft embrace in the chaotic world around them.

As the sun began to set, painting the sky in hues of orange and rose, they stood still, suspended in that moment. It was a declaration of their hidden emotions, reflecting back at them a truth they both had feared to acknowledge. Mahmoud reached out, brushing a stray lock of Leila's hair behind her ear, a gesture both tender and revealing. The space between them pulsed with unspoken promises, solidifying their longing for one another. With the stars beginning to twinkle above, Leila whispered:

"Perhaps this is not just a moment but the beginning of something extraordinary."

Their eyes locked once more, a silent vow passed between them, igniting hope for the paths they might walk together. Connecting their lives, they shaped a story destined to unfold across Paris, Tunis, and beyond, each chapter steeped in the beautiful suspense of their evolving love.

Chapter 4

The Dance of Shadows

The chandeliers, twinkling like stars trapped in crystal, cast soft light on the polished wood floors. Canvases adorned with vibrant splashes of color hang like secrets, whispering stories of love and loss. Conversations swirl around Leila and Mahmoud, their laughter mingling with the strains of a distant piano. As they weave through the crowd, the air thickens with the scent of expensive perfume and aged wine, creating an intoxicating atmosphere that both invigorates and ensnares.

Leila, with her fiery red hair that dances like flames, catches the eye of those around her, blending beauty and mystery. Mahmoud, the learned professor, carries a quiet strength, his gaze scanning the room for the familiar spark of Leila's laughter. Their glances are ephemeral but charged, a magnetic connection that ignites even the most mundane moment.

"You must tell me about your dreams, Leila," he whispers, his voice barely above the hum of conversation.

She responds with a teasing smile:

"And you must show me the poetry hidden in your soul."

With each passing moment, the thrill of possibility hangs between them, like the promise of a profound revelation waiting to unfold.

* * *

Each stolen glance carries a weight, as Leila and Mahmoud attempt to mask their growing affection. In the dim light of the lecture hall, shadows dance between them like the secrets they dare not share. Leila, with her fiery red hair cascading like a flame against her porcelain skin, sits in the front row, scribbling notes that she may never look at again. Every fleeting moment when she looks up, her green eyes lock onto Mahmoud's, igniting sparks that thread through the room. He returns her gaze, his dark eyes reflecting a depth she longs to explore, yet he retreats behind a façade of professionalism. Outside, Paris' bustle fades away into mere background noise as their silent conversation intensifies; each glance exchanges unspoken words, weaving a tapestry of feelings that neither is brave enough to articulate.

After class, the corridor between them feels like a vast ocean, yet every step brings her closer to him. Outside, the vibrant colors of the Seine mirror the heat of their unacknowledged emotions; the bridge connecting two worlds, much like the connection they share. Mahmoud, a seasoned professor at thirty-six, finds himself captivated by the audacity of her youth and the brilliance of her insight.

"What did you think of Baudelaire?" he asks, an open invitation coated in soft urgency.

Leila's heart races as she responds:

"Perhaps the beauty lies not just in the words, but in the spaces between them."

Their laughter dances in the air, a sweet melody that lingers long after their voices fade, leaving behind an echo of feelings that pulse like the heartbeat of the city around them.

* * *

The lively dance floor pulsed with energy, lights shimmering like stars trapped in a crystal globe. Leila, with her flaming red hair cascading like a fiery waterfall over her shoulders, twirled among an ocean of twinkling laughter and discreet whispers. Each rhythm brought her closer to Mahmoud, the professor whose deep, knowing eyes held the mystery of ancient texts and forgotten tales. As they moved together, her heart beat in time with the drumming music, a captivating force that made the surrounding world dissolve into a dreamy haze. Together, they lost themselves, entrusting their souls to the cadence that turned the night into a vivid tapestry of emotions.

Amidst the swirling colors, their bodies became entwined, each step a promise of unspoken desires. The air thickened with unvoiced thoughts as they danced through moments both fleeting and eternal. Mahmoud leaned closer, his voice barely a whisper above the melody:

"Do you feel it, Leila? Our souls; two stories crossing paths."

The thrill of his words sent a shiver down her spine, igniting a longing she couldn't quite comprehend. With every twirl, they collided, like stars in the night sky, illuminating the space between them. The laughter of others faded, making way for the magnetic pull of their connection. Each movement became an uncharted territory they were willing to explore, full of potential and promise, adding to the tapestry of their shared moment; one rich with intimacy and suspense.

Chapter 5

The City of Dreams

The morning sun casts a golden glow over the ancient buildings as she steps onto the cobblestone streets, her red hair catching the light like a flame. Each brick seems to whisper secrets of the past, each shadow dances with the echoes of long-forgotten tales. She strolls past the Tower of London, its imposing walls a steadfast guardian of centuries-old secrets, and feels an inexplicable urge to touch the cold stone, as if such an act might forge a link with the stories etched into its history. What stories do you hold? she murmurs to the tower, a playful smile on her lips, inviting the silence to answer.

As she wanders through the city, Leila dreams of Mahmoud. The bustle of the market blends with the haunting melody of his voice reciting verses of classic literature, leaving her with a bittersweet ache in her chest. She imagines him beside her, his presence palpable at every landmark, his laughter resonating in her ears like the chiming of Big Ben.

"You would love this place," she whispers to the air, her heart swelling with the blend of longing and hope.

Each stop; the British Museum, the serene banks of the Thames; feels like a page from a story they have yet to write together. The city, with its mysterious charm, cradles her dreams. It wraps around her like a tender embrace, promising that one day soon, their destinies will intertwine once again, sweeping them into a beautiful, unexpected adventure.

* * *

In a cozy bookstore tucked away in the heart of Paris, Leila often found solace among the pages. The scent of old books blended with fresh coffee lingered in the air, inviting her to lose herself in tales of love and longing. With fiery red hair cascading down her shoulders, she was an unmistakable presence. Every visit was an escape from the pulse of the city, where her mind could wander freely through the labyrinths of love that filled the shelves. She often imagined herself as the heroine navigating romance like the characters she read about, dreaming of serendipitous meetings and whispered words.

One afternoon, while browsing through a collection of poetry, an unexpected sighting caught her eye. Mahmoud, her professor of Arab literature, stood by a large window, sunlight framing his silhouette. His presence ignited a flutter in her chest, a mix of hope and fevered anticipation that coursed through her veins. She remembered the way he spoke about the intricacies of love in literature, his voice rich with passion, and suddenly those lessons felt like prophecies written just for her. As he turned, their eyes locked for a fleeting moment, and time seemed to stand still. Her heart raced as if the words of her favorite novels danced to life, intertwining their fates for a brief breath of possibility.

The air thickened with unspoken words, electrifying the space between them, as they exchanged casual pleasantries.

"Did you find any treasures today, Leila?" he asked, a smile playing at the corners of his lips.

She felt her cheeks flush, the warmth of his gaze anchoring her within this moment.

"Always," she managed to reply, her voice barely above a whisper, the weight of his attention weaving a spell around them.

In that tiny world of literature, surrounded by stories that promised love and adventure, hope blossomed anew. Their connection lingered like the closing pages of a beloved book, teasing her with the sweet promise of what could unfold if only she dared to turn the page.

* * *

The sun dipped low over the rooftops of Paris, casting a warm glow that danced through the leaves of the trees lining the boulevard. Leila's heart fluttered with anticipation as she arrived at their rendezvous point, a quaint café nestled in the heart of Montmartre. She smoothed her red hair over her shoulders, searching for Mahmoud among the bustling tables. His presence made her skin tingle, like whispers of wind promising the unknown. They greeted each other with a knowing smile, the unspoken bond of shared dreams and aspirations hovering in the air between them.

As they stepped out into the winding streets, the world transformed into a canvas of colors and sounds that sparked their imaginations. They meandered through narrow alleys adorned with ivy, each corner revealing a cherished secret of the city.

"Do you ever think about the stories we have yet to live?" Leila asked, her voice soft and curious.

Mahmoud paused, turning to meet her emerald gaze, his brow furrowing in thought.

"Every moment, Leila," he replied, "is a page waiting to be written."

With each step, their whispered intentions intertwined, creating a narrative too intricate to unravel. The streets seemed to echo their fears and dreams, and together, they loomed over possibilities waiting to unfold.

The city pulsated around them as they wove through the labyrinth of Paris, an invisible thread binding their fates. Voices of distant laughter filled the air, mingling with the sound of footsteps and the gentle clinking of glasses.

"I have always wanted to visit Cairo," Leila confided, a shy smile brushing her lips as they crossed a bridge over the Seine.

Mahmoud nodded, a spark igniting in his chest.

"It is rich with stories," he said. "Just like you."

Their laughter drifted like music in the evening breeze, thick with the promise of adventure. In that moment, against the backdrop of twinkling lights reflected on the water, they chose to embrace uncertainty, converting whispers into words and dreams into journeys.

Chapter 6

Echoes of Cairo

The vibrant chaos shimmers beneath the golden sun, where vendors call out, and scents of spices mingle with the cool breeze. Each corner hides whispers of love and heartbreak, legends etched into the stones worn smooth by countless footsteps. The architecture, a tapestry woven through centuries, stands as a testament to the lives lived within its embrace. As Leila walked alongside Mahmoud, she felt the pulse of the city, transforming it into a canvas alive with color and sound. With each step, they surrendered to the rhythm, their hearts entwined by the history echoing through the alleyways, urging them to follow the traces of those who came before.

She glances at Mahmoud, his eyes reflecting the wisdom of ages past.

"Does this place speak to you?" she asks, her voice barely above a whisper, filled with a mixture of curiosity and awe.

He smiles, his gaze lingering on the intricacies of an ornate door, a gateway to a time forgotten.

"Every stone, every shadow holds a secret," he replies softly, intertwining his fingers with hers. "Our love, like this city, has endured turmoil; yet it blossoms amidst chaos."

The sunset casts a surreal glow, enveloping them in warmth, as if the universe conspired to celebrate their bond. In that moment, amidst historical echoes and unspoken promises, they found solace, knowing that both the streets of Cairo and their hearts bore witness to a love that would transcend time.

As they continued their exploration, it became clear that the past was not merely a remote ghost but an active participant in their journey, reminding them that love, like history, is a tapestry of moments stitched together with threads of resilience and hope. Both Leila and Mahmoud understood that they were destined to wander, to embrace the stories that shaped them; as intertwined as the patterns in the ancient mosaic beneath their feet. It is crucial to remember that every city carries the weight of its stories, urging those who traverse its path to be open to the magic hidden in the mundane. This allows the heart to grow, nurturing love that withstands the sands of time.

* * *

The rooftop dinner set the stage, an intimate escape high above the bustling streets of Paris. As Leila and Mahmoud sat beneath a canopy of stars, the city lights sparkled below, mirroring the flickering hopes and dreams each held tightly within. The food was exquisite, a fusion of flavors from both Tunisia and France, but it was the atmosphere that drew them closer. Laughter mingled with soft whispers as they stole glances at each other, feeling the electric pull of unspoken words.

"Do you see them?" Leila pointed to the distant lights, her voice a gentle melody. "Those are our dreams, shining bright yet so far away." Mahmoud nodded, a hint of a smile playing on his lips. "And like the stars, they guide us, even if we can't touch them."

As they settled into the warmth of the evening, the world below faded away, leaving just the two of them, the gentle breeze weaving through their thoughts. They shared tales of hope; Leila spoke of her childhood summers in Tunis, how the sun would paint the landscape in golden hues, and how she longed to make her mark in the world. Mahmoud listened intently, captivated not just by her words but by the vulnerability that flickered in her green eyes.

"Sometimes I feel like I am just a bridge," he shared, his gaze drifting to the shimmering horizon. "Connecting my passion for literature with my students, yet fearing what lies on the other side."

The air thickened with emotion, the night wrapping around them like a comforting embrace. In the silence, their hands found each other, fingers entwining as if acknowledging the fragility of their confessions. Beneath the vast expanse of stars, a promise lingered; of honesty, of dreams shared, and the potential of a love that could bridge the distance between their worlds.

* * *

In a moment of courage, Mahmoud stepped into the cloistered calm of the small café, a narrow space tucked away in the winding streets of Montmartre. The aroma of freshly brewed coffee wrapped around him like an embrace, yet his heart raced with unsteady beats. Outside, the Parisian twilight spilled through the window, casting a gentle glow on Leila's red hair, which caught the light like flames dancing amidst the shadows. He had spent so many nights pondering his feelings, fears swirling like autumn leaves. The air felt charged, electric, as he locked eyes with her.

"Leila," he began, his voice trembling slightly, "there's something I need to tell you." He swallowed hard, every word an ocean tide crashing against his insecurities. "I cannot deny it any longer. You have captivated me in ways I never thought possible."

As the words unfolded, he could see her surprise morph into something deeper, a flicker of understanding that mirrored his own vulnerability.

Their hearts united in an honest confession, solidifying the bond formed through shared words. Leila leaned forward, her emerald eyes like windows to her soul.

"Mahmoud, I have felt an impossible attraction, a thread pulling us together through the cacophony of our lives. It felt reckless, yet inevitable."

The café faded around them, replaced by a cocoon of warmth and promise. Each confession interwove their pasts, their dreams, and in that moment, Paris became their own enchanted realm. The laughter of patrons, the clinking of cups, all faded, as they shared secrets draped in the luminescence of truth. They spoke of origins, of burdens, of hopes, peeling back layers of pretense to reveal an undeniable bond; a connection that transcended age, culture, and circumstance. In that sacred space, they discovered not only their desires but also a mutual respect that had long been buried beneath the weight of unspoken words. It was a moment etched forever in their memory, a vow sewn deeply into the fabric of their lives.

Chapter 7

Mirage of Feelings

The skyline, a jagged silhouette against the azure sky, glimmers with the promise of dreams yet unfulfilled. Leila, with her fierce red hair billowing in the warm, perfumed breeze, felt as if she were wandering through a modern fairy tale. Each towering building whispered secrets of ambition and heartbreak while the golden sands flowed beneath her feet, symbolizing time slipping away. Mahmoud, standing beside her, embodied the weight of knowledge and the wonder of discovery. His deep voice broke the enchanting silence, There is a beauty here, Leila, that is both breathtaking and bewildering. She glanced at him, her emerald eyes reflecting a myriad of emotions. It feels like the world is holding its breath, she replied softly, unaware that their journey was about to dive deeper into the essence of their connection.

Each twist and turn in the opulent streets seems to pull them closer, as if the universe conspired to weave their destinies together. They wandered through the bustling souks, where colors burst forth like the petals of a blooming flower, and scents of spices danced around them like ethereal spirits. Mahmoud shared tales of ancient poets who found love amidst such beauty, and Leila listened, captivated, as his words painted vivid pictures in her mind. Do you believe in serendipity? she asked, her heart pounding with vulnerability. He paused, meeting her gaze, the flickering lights of the city mirrored in his warm brown eyes. Every moment in this city feels like a serendipitous brush with destiny. The air thickened with the promise of something more, a bond forged by laughter, shared struggles, and whispered dreams beneath the starlit sky.

In the heart of Dubai, amidst the extravagant manifestos of architecture, they discovered a world where barriers melted away. Here, beneath the opalescent moon, their love flourished, wild and unrestrained, like the evening breeze that kissed their cheeks. They sought adventure together, conquering dunes and scaling heights, yet it was in the stillness of shared silences that their hearts truly spoke. The moment Mahmoud took Leila's hand, entwining their fingers, transformed the ordinary into the extraordinary. It was a simple act yet filled with promise, a preamble to a happy ending waiting to unfold. In a city where dreams were built, they began to construct a narrative of their own; a story marked by enchantment, rich with the textures of longing, joy, and passion. If you ever find yourself wandering through Dubai, pause and allow the beauty of your surroundings to reflect the depths of your heart. Embrace the journey of love, for it is often where the finest adventures lie.

* * *

Overlooking the majestic Burj Khalifa, Leila felt the gentle breeze play with her fiery red hair, each strand dancing like a wild flame caught in an enchanting game. Mahmoud stood beside her, his gaze lost in the silhouette of the towering structure that pierced the Dubai sky, mirroring the aspirations pulsing between them. The city sparkled below; a dazzling tapestry woven with whispers of prosperity and dreams. It was a moment suspended in time, filled with an electric hope that radiated from their hearts, hinting at futures intertwined, threads within a vast fabric of possibility. They exchanged glances, each reflecting a mix of excitement and trepidation, knowing the paths of their lives had converged in this very instant.

The grandeur of the moment enveloped them, lifting their spirits to heights they had only dared to imagine. Do you think love can reach such heights? Leila's voice was barely above a whisper, as if the city below might hear her secret wish. Mahmoud turned to her, his dark eyes glistening with understanding. If it is true love, it knows no bounds, he replied, his voice rich like the literature he cherished. They stood together, united against the skyline, pondering the infinity of their potential. As the Burj Khalifa sparkled in the twilight, an emblem of dreams realized, they glimpsed a future glowing with promise; a life steeped in passion and boundless exploration. In that moment, beneath the star-studded sky, they felt their love ascend, as if it could touch the stars.

* * *

In the heart of Dubai's vibrant markets, where exotic spices mingle with the echoes of laughter and whispers of dreams, Leila and Mahmoud find themselves drawn into a shared fantasy. The stalls overflowed with vibrant textiles and delicate trinkets, promising stories untold. Leila, her red hair a fiery beacon, scouted the treasures hidden among the shadows. She felt enchanted by the bustling energy surrounding her, a fervent symphony resonating through the air. Mahmoud, observing her delight, couldn't help but feel his heart dance with her.

"What do you see?" he asked, his voice a gentle caress against the backdrop of the marketplace.

"A world where we can be more than ourselves," she replied, her eyes reflecting a universe of dreams.

In that fleeting moment, their shared aspirations seemed to magnify the space around them, weaving their fantasies into an iridescent tapestry of hope.

As they journey through the labyrinthine streets of Dubai, their souls converge in ways that rival the grandeur of the cities they traverse. Each alley they wander seems to mirror the turning pages of a story yet to be written. Mahmoud speaks of the poets who roamed these lands, while Leila listens, her heart swelling with admiration. The age difference between them fades amidst the weave of their connection, shadows of doubt and fear left behind at the thresholds of their converging destinies.

"Does the heart know age?" Mahmoud mused, catching her gaze in a lingering embrace.

"Perhaps it only knows the essence of what truly matters," she answered, the weight of their collective journey making her words resonate deeply.

As the sun dipped below the skyline, painting the city in hues of gold, they realized that their paths had entwined, forging a shared destiny illuminated by the warmth of their entwined souls.

With each exchange, they ventured deeper not just into the labyrinth of markets but into the very essence of themselves, unearthing layers long buried by time and expectation. Every laugh, every whispered secret echoed in the air like an incantation, drawing them closer until no distance seemed great enough to separate them. Their love blossomed silently beneath the backdrop of vibrant cityscapes, whispered in the winds that danced through the streets. The stories of old towns felt alive in their shared breaths, creating a unity that stemmed from their quests and dreams. Therein lies a practical revelation in their narrative; love does not merely thrive in the grand moments but flourishes in the simple revelations under starlit skies or amidst the chaos of a market, where two souls can converge to create a world of endless possibilities.

Chapter 8

The Crossroads

As their lives intertwined further, dilemmas began to emerge, testing the very essence of Leila and Mahmoud's love. In the enchanting streets of Paris, where history whispered through the cobblestones, a delicate balance hung in the air. Each moment they spent together was filled with laughter and poetry, yet beneath the surface simmered a fierce undercurrent of choices waiting to rise. Would their love withstand the influence of family expectations and societal norms? Mahmoud, with his seasoned heart, cherished Leila's vibrant red hair, its fiery hue a stark contrast to his own contemplative nature, yet he feared the shadows their secrets cast. Leila, caught between her father's ambitions and her own desires, struggled to find her voice in a world that often spoke for her. The allure of romance tinged with uncertainty lingered in the corners of their shared glances, where words remained unspoken, and the truth threatened to spill over.

Every decision felt heavy, with the past looming larger like a forgotten story begging to be told. As they explored the bustling markets of Tunis and the scenic vistas of Cairo, every choice was laced with memories, each intertwined with the profound question of what love truly meant. Mahmoud often found himself pondering the sacrifices they had to face. What if my past becomes your chain? he quietly asked her one evening under the stars. Leila's eyes glistened like the pavements of Paris after rain as she replied, But what if love is our freedom? The tension between duty and passion curled around them, wrapping them in a cocoon of anticipation. The next crossroads awaited them in London, where their lives would intersect again, each choice drawing them closer to an ultimate revelation.

As they continued their journey, the allure of Dubai shimmered like a mirage on the horizon, full of promise yet fraught with impending choices. Their dreams danced in the twilight as they wrestled with the haunting echoes of their decisions. Yet amidst the chaos, their love flourished; an emerald garden blossoming in the desert. They discovered that sometimes, the weight of choices could turn burdens into wings. A secret pact was forged during a quiet moment, sealing their decision to embrace whatever lay ahead together. In this intricate tapestry of love and longing, they learned the most crucial lesson: that true commitment lies not in the absence of dilemmas, but in the courage to choose each other, time and again, against all odds.

** * **

Leila stepped into the gallery, her red hair catching the subtle glow of the chandeliers. The air was thick with the scent of oil paint and linseed, a familiar comfort that wrapped around her like a warm shawl. But today, the allure of art left her feeling restless. She drifted past canvases splashed with vibrant hues but found no solace within the strokes. Each piece felt like a mirror reflecting her uncertainties about the future. Canvases that depicted worlds beyond her own – bold cities, forlorn lovers, distant lands. Her heart was a canvas too, filled with emotions she couldn't quite articulate. A sense of impending change lingered around her like shadows in a dimly-lit room, as if the paintings whispered secrets of untraveled paths yet to unfold.

Just as she decided to retreat into the solace of a quiet corner, a familiar voice broke through the hum of conversations.

"Leila?"

Mahmoud stood before her, framed by the soft light filtering through the gallery windows. Time had morphed him into a more rustic version of the man she remembered. Those deep-set eyes, now touched with hints of worry, still held the same warmth.

"What are you doing here?" he asked, stepping closer, curiosity mixed with a hint of surprise.

His presence triggered a rush of memories wrapped in nuances of their past interactions – each lecture in the grandeur of the Sorbonne, their spirited debates about literature, but also the silence that loomed large between them, unspoken words heavy in the air. This encounter, unexpected as it was, soon turned into a test of the bond that tethered them both; a connection that felt deeper than mere student and teacher, yet held back by the constraints of their roles.

They meandered through the gallery, sharing stolen glances and tentative smiles as the world faded around them. It was as if they had created their own enclave amid the sea of strangers.

"Do you remember reading 'One Hundred Years of Solitude'?" Mahmoud asked, voice low and intimate, drawing her into a world of magic and memory. "I can still see you scribbling furiously in your notebook."

The warmth that fluttered in her chest grew, intertwining with the questions threading through her mind. Could something more than friendship blossom from the ashes of their missed opportunities? Leila caught her breath, and in that moment, she realized that perhaps it was not the gallery around them that held the art of life, but the uncharted territory of what remained unspoken between them. And beneath the surface of their delicate tension, a promise lingered – a promise that despite the odds of age, background, and differences, a new story was poised to unfold.

* * *

Amidst the clamor of Paris streets, where life thrummed with unyielding energy, Mahmoud and Leila stood at the edge of a bustling café, the scent of fresh croissants mingling with the cool autumn air. The world outside faded as they locked eyes, his deep-set gaze searching the mysteries woven into her fiery red hair.

"Whatever may come," he whispered, "we shall face it together."

The weight of his promise filled the spaces between them, a tangible force that pushed back against the chaos encircling their lives.

Leila, her heart racing, let her fingers caress the pages of the poetry collection nestled in her satchel, filled with verses that echoed their own unraveling tale.

"I believe you," she murmured, her voice low and intimate, a spell shared under the watchful gaze of shadows.

Their vows were not mere words; they tethered them to a shared journey stretching across continents; from the narrow streets of Tunis to the pulsating heart of Dubai. Each promise was a thread, intricately woven into their story, a binding declaration of faith in the face of uncertainty.

In the quiet corners of late-night discussions, their hearts poured forth unanswered questions, dreams, and fears.

"You have changed my perception of love," she said, eyes shining like amber jewels.

They found solace in each other's whispers, reminding themselves that every challenge they faced was but a chapter in a novel not yet finished. As their laughter intertwined like a soft melody, they knew they would turn the pages together, writing an ending where hope resided. Through the maze of uncertainty, there was a truth they clung to; their love was a universe vast enough to embrace it all.

Chapter 9

The Threads of Destiny

Leila stood at the edge of her father's opulent Parisian terrace, the evening breeze brushing against her fiery red hair, whispering secrets of her desires and fears. At just twenty-three, she felt the heavy weight of expectation pressing down upon her. The romantic dimness of sunset painted the skyline in shades of gold and indigo, yet her heart was tangled in shadows. Her mind danced between the laughter and warmth of Mahmoud, her enchanting professor, and the steadfast path laid out before her by her father, an ambitious entrepreneur with grand visions for his daughter. Love and obligation warred within her, each pulling her in a different direction.

Memories of their shared moments flickered in her mind like the lights of Paris at night; the way his voice floated over the verses of ancient poets and how his eyes sparkled with passion when speaking of literature. She could almost feel him beside her, his presence bringing both comfort and turmoil. 'Leila,' he had said during their last lecture, 'true fulfillment lies in choosing what ignites the very essence of your soul, not in adhering to the chains of expectation.' His words echoed in her mind like a haunting melody, begging for her to listen as she peered into an uncertain future.

A sudden realization jolted her from her reverie, striking like a bolt of lightning through the dusk. What if she was meant for more than the life prescribed to her? What if love was the answer she had been seeking? The thought of losing Mahmoud; a man who saw the world beyond the text and understood her more deeply than anyone; sent a rush of exhilaration through her veins. She felt courage surging within her. In that moment, the temptation to follow her heart over obligation transformed into a fierce determination. As she gazed across the Paris skyline, the choice became clearer, illuminated by the glow of the Eiffel Tower in the distance. A leap of faith awaited her, ready to embrace the unpredictable yet thrilling adventure ahead, and with it, the chance to seize her own destiny.

With newfound resolve, Leila knew she had to speak her truth. The next day, she found herself standing outside Mahmoud's office at the Sorbonne, heart racing and palms clammy. She knocked, and as the door creaked open, she was greeted by his familiar smile. In the solace of his presence, she let her walls fall. Words spilled forth like poetry, potent and honest.

"I want to explore the world with you, not just the pages of books," she confessed, her voice trembling yet clear.

Mahmoud's gaze softened, and he stepped closer, enveloping her in a warmth that melted her fears.

"Then let's embark on this journey together, Leila. Love conquers all borders," he whispered, sealing their fate with a promise that shimmered like starlight across the vast expanse of their future.

* * *

In a quiet corner of a bustling Paris café, sunlight danced through the ornate balcony, casting playful shadows on their faces. Leila's striking red hair glowed like embers in the soft light, but her eyes betrayed a tempest of emotions. Mahmoud, always composed, found his heart racing with every breath he took beside her. Their conversation began with casual references to literature and art, but soon shifted to something deeper, something raw and vulnerable. With each word, they chipped away at the façades they had constructed, forging a bridge of sincerity that demanded their secret fears and aspirations to step into the light.

"You think love is enough?" she asked, her voice trembling slightly, revealing cracks in her confident demeanor.

Mahmoud shifted in his seat, the weight of silence pressing against him.

"Love is a journey," he whispered. "But it requires trust."

It was in that moment; when the truth hung heavy in the air; that they began to uncover the uncharted territories of their souls.

As they spoke, an electric tension knit itself between them; their vulnerabilities merged, revealing the profound depth of their feelings. They shared stories of childhood; Leila's endless dreams of living freely, untethered by expectations; Mahmoud's labored path through academia, colored by a longing for acceptance. The blinding layers of misunderstanding and restraint began to dissolve, paving the way for intimacy.

"I've long admired your spirit, Leila," Mahmoud confessed, his gaze steady.

Her cheeks flushed at his admission, a blend of surprise and warmth that ignited something buried within her.

"And I have always felt that there's more to you than just a professor," she replied, the mystery of his world drawing her closer.

They stood on the precipice of discovery, the walls of their hearts peeling away, revealing a landscape rich with emotions they had too often concealed. In that sacred space, they glimpsed the possibility of something greater; a love that could thrive amidst the chaos of their lives, resonating like poetry that had yet to be penned.

As twilight draped the skyline of Paris in a dusky embrace, they both realized that they stood not just as teacher and student, but as two kindred spirits, each forging the path not only to one another's hearts but also to their own truths. The journey ahead was uncertain, marked by the shadows of their pasts and the unknown possibilities of their future. Leila took Mahmoud's hand, the warmth radiating between them a quiet promise.

"Let's not fear what lies ahead," she said, her eyes sparkling with an adventurous spirit.

Mahmoud smiled, a sense of hope igniting within him. With the enchanting city bearing witness, they stepped into the future hand in hand, ready to face whatever challenges awaited them. Their hearts, now unshackled, beat in unison to the rhythm of love newly discovered, an authentic connection promising that true feelings, once confronted, can illuminate even the darkest paths.

* * *

As secrets spill forth like a cascading spring, clarity emerges in the midst of a fog that enveloped Leila and Mahmoud for too long. The air in the small café along the banks of the Seine feels charged, electric, as Leila's red hair catches the afternoon light, making her look like a flame dancing in the midst of a dark room where shadows usually lurk. Mahmoud watches her, his heart caught in a whirlwind of desperation and hope. I always knew there was more beneath the surface, he whispers, each word laced with truth as he sips his espresso, its bitterness balancing the sweetness of his growing affection for her. You are like a hidden gem, he continues, revealing layers of understanding that were once obscured by misconceptions and fears. The murmur of Paris drifts through the window, carrying with it the whispers of their pasts, weaving a tale that had somehow defied the efforts of time and distance to tear them apart.

The tangled threads of Lebanese culture run through them, intertwining their identities like the intricate patterns of lace made in the streets of Beirut. For Leila, embodying her father's Tunisian roots while growing up in the vibrancy of Paris has shaped her views of love and belonging. With every word she exchanges with Mahmoud, who carries the weight of academic tradition on his shoulders and the warmth of his heritage in his heart, the essence of her love for him illuminates her very being.

"You taught me that literature holds the keys to the universe," she says, her voice a melody, each note resonating with unspoken desires.

Mahmoud's gaze captures hers, drawing them closer, as if the miles between Cairo and London had shrunk to nothing, and their souls were now free to dance together in a world of endless possibilities. The suspense of the unknown hangs between them, but it is a mystery worth unraveling together, a shared journey to unearth the depth of their connection.

Chapter 10

A New Beginning

The echoes of their previous lives faded with each step they took along the River Seine, where the soft murmur of water and distant laughter mingled in the evening air. Leila's red hair flickered like a lighthouse against the twilight, drawing Mahmoud's gaze as they strolled hand in hand, their fingers entwined in a secret pact of love and hope. Paris feels different today, she whispered, her eyes sparkling with anticipation. Mahmoud looked at her, his heart swelling. It feels like the world is ours to create, he replied, a hint of mischief dancing in his tone.

The cobblestone streets shimmered under the low glow of the streetlamps, casting shadows that seemed to dance along with them. Every café they passed held stories of lovers and poets, their shared whispers enveloping Leila and Mahmoud like a soft embrace. In that moment, they were unwritten pages, eager for ink. Mahmoud tightened his grip on Leila as they paused before an art gallery displaying vibrant paintings that spoke of distant lands and uncharted emotions.

"Shall we?" he asked, nodding towards the entrance.

Leila's smile radiated warmth, and with a gentle squeeze, they crossed the threshold together, stepping into a world painted with the hues of possibility.

In a hidden corner of the gallery, they stumbled upon a painting of two souls intertwined, lost in a moment suspended in time. The colors bled into one another, capturing a passion that transcended words. Leila leaned closer, captivated by the depth of the artwork.

"It reminds me of us," she breathed, her voice barely above a whisper.

Mahmoud, gazing into her vivid eyes, felt time pause.

"A tapestry woven by fate," he mused, imagining their journey through the bustling streets of Paris, the serene northern suburbs of Tunis, the vibrant chaos of Cairo, and the glitzy horizons of Dubai.

Each destination was a chapter waiting to be written, a saga of love interlaced with discovery. The night air buzzed with the fragrance of possibility, enveloping them like a spell. They stepped back outside, hearts synchronized with the rhythm of the city. In that enchanted moment, they knew; with every heartbeat; that the past no longer defined them. The future sparkled ahead, waiting for their next brushstroke on this new canvas.

* * *

Friends gathered in the softly-lit courtyard of a charming Parisian café, where the evening air was imbued with the warmth of laughter and an unspoken promise. Tables were adorned with delicate wildflowers, their simple beauty echoing the vibrant spirit of the love being celebrated. Leila, her red hair catching the light like a flame dancing in the evening breeze, moved gracefully among the guests. Mahmoud, with his quiet intensity, stood slightly apart, observing the joyous chaos with a mixture of pride and awe.

"Can you believe it? We did it!" Leila's voice rang out, a blend of excitement and disbelief.

Mahmoud chuckled softly, his eyes twinkling:

"Love has a way of writing its own stories."

As the night deepened, Mahmud reflected on their union; a tapestry woven from threads of culture, literature, and passion. Each moment felt like a line from a beloved novel, alive with the color of adventures from Parisian streets to Tunisian shores. Their connection blossomed like the jasmine flowers so often found in the streets of Cairo.

"You are my muse, Leila," he whispered, pulling her closer amidst the laughter and chatter.

She smiled, her heart stirring with a mix of dreams and reality:

"And you are the pen that writes my heart's poetry."

Together they created a resonance that seemed to echo through the ages, a beautiful blend of their worlds.

With every toast made, the night swirled into a rich tapestry of memories being forged. Friends recounted stories of love and longing, each one a brushstroke on the canvas of that magical evening. In this celebration, a sense of belonging enveloped them like a warm blanket. Mahmoud glanced at Leila, who was now animatedly recounting tales from her studies, her passion infectious. The thrill of their collective journey was palpable. As the clock struck midnight, hands intertwined, they were reminded that love, in its myriad forms, was the greatest adventure of all; a quest that transcended borders and bridged cultures, promising a joyful horizon ahead, one filled with endless possibility.

* * *

In a moment of quiet, under the soft glow of a Parisian café light, Leila and Mahmoud found themselves enveloped in a world that was theirs alone. The bustling noise of the city faded away, replaced by a silence that felt sacred, almost reverent. I promise to nurture what we have, come what may, Mahmoud whispered, his voice barely above the rustle of the evening breeze. The words hung in the air, filled with a weight that spoke of commitment and tenderness. Leila's red hair caught the glint of the street lamps, dancing like flames around her face as she nodded, her heart echoing his promise.

Their hearts intertwined like verses of poetry, each heartbeat a stanza that attested to their unique connection. As they gazed into each other's eyes, time itself seemed to yield, a silent witness to the depth of their bond.

"Do you feel it, Mahmoud?" Leila asked softly, a hint of mystery in her voice. "Our love is like the stories we read, transcending the boundaries of pages and ink."

He smiled, taking her hand, feeling the warmth radiate between their skin. Across cities; Tunis, London, Cairo, and even the glittering towers of Dubai; they could sense the threads of their destiny weaving tighter, affirming that this love story was just beginning, a tale to be written in the stars.

As the evening drew to a close, they stepped into the night, ready to face whatever challenges life would present them. They had each other, and that was enough. The streets of Paris shimmered with possibilities, and the world awaited their story. Each step echoed with the promise of adventure and the assurance that love, in its purest form, is an eternal bond that can withstand the test of time and distances. Nurturing this connection became their purpose, a tangible note in the composition of their lives, inviting them to explore not just each other but the world around them.

PART TWO

The Mystery of The Red Man

Chapter 11

The First Whisper

The neighborhood on the outskirts of Paris seemed asleep, its quiet cloaking every inch in a sense of calm that felt just a little too perfect. Houses sat neatly side by side, their windows dark, each yard empty except for the shadows of rustling trees. Dubois parked his car at the curb, eyes darting across the street as if expecting someone to emerge from the darkness at any moment. It was a scene that could have been taken from any suburban postcard, yet beneath the stillness, he sensed something was wrong. His instincts, sharpened over years of investigating dark corners, prickled with unease. A broken window, a flickering streetlamp, or even the faintest whisper of movement might be enough to shatter this fragile veneer of peace.

He stepped out, closing the door quietly behind him, and felt the weight of silence pressing down. Usually, there would be faint sounds: children's laughter, neighbors chatting, the distant hum of daily life. Tonight, though, all that remained was an oppressive stillness.

As Dubois moved down the street toward the house that had been the center of recent disturbances, his mind raced through prior reports. Small anomalies that, taken alone, seemed trivial: a found candle, strange symbols carved into the mud, or a flickering light that appeared and vanished without explanation. Tonight, those pieces finally made less sense; they felt like fragments of a larger picture, one that was slowly coming into focus as darker and more disturbing than he had originally believed.

The house itself looked abandoned. The door was ajar, hinges creaking softly with each breeze. An acrid smell of burnt wax and dampness drifted from within. Carefully, Dubois pushed the door open and stepped inside, his eyes adjusting to the dimness.

The interior was silent, save for a faint, rhythmic ticking coming from somewhere deeper inside; the kind of sound that made the hairs on his neck stand on end. The living room was strewn with debris, pages torn from books, and strange markings scrawled onto the walls in red ink that looked more like blood. His gaze settled on a long, dark stain spreading from the center of the room; a stark reminder of something violent, something beyond simple vandalism. The silence here seemed unnervingly thick, as if the house was holding its breath, waiting for something to shatter it.

But it wasn't until he reached the back of the house that Dubois found what truly unsettled him. Behind a heavy curtain, hidden from casual view, was a small altar; a crude wooden table covered with symbols and objects that defied explanation. An ancient-looking candle, unburnt but coated with layers of dust, sat beside a cluster of flat stones engraved with runes. Nearby, a torn photograph of a young woman, face mostly obscured, was pinned to the wall with a rusty knife. The entire scene radiated an aura of ritual, of something deliberately left behind. His fingers trembled slightly as he took out his phone, into which he snapped pictures, trying to hold onto the image even as unease prickled deeper into his chest. Whatever was happening here, it was rooted in something much darker; something with history, with tradition, and with blood spilled long ago.

As Dubois examined the symbols, a faint, distant whisper seemed to drift through the house; a faint echo of something long forgotten. The stillness, once oppressive, now felt alive, as if the house itself was responding. His mind flashed back to Elise's research; a scholar specializing in local legends and ancient rites. She had warned him about the dark history of the village, about a ritual that had supposedly been performed centuries ago, when the land was torn apart by greed and betrayal. Now, standing at the heart of this macabre scene, he realized that whatever had begun here was far from over. The silence wasn't just the absence of noise; it was a warning. Something had been awakened, and it was waiting. Waiting to make its next move; and Dubois couldn't shake the feeling that he was already too late to stop it.

Chapter 12

The Phantom's Calling Card

The evening was routine until the call came in. A neighbor had reported seeing a missing person poster tucked beneath a pile of newspapers on the porch of a quiet suburban house. Normally, these incidents barely flicked a flicker in Detective Julien Dubois's mind, but something about this one felt off. The poster was recent, fresh even, with a grainy photograph of a young woman whose eyes seemed to stare directly at him through the cracked paper. As he approached the house, the fading sunset cast long shadows over the neatly trimmed lawns, contrasting sharply with the feeling that something had quietly unraveled behind the windows.

Inside, the house was eerily silent. Nothing seemed disturbed; no signs of struggle, no overturned furniture. Just a blanket of calm masking a dark hole in its core. Julien's eyes lingered on the photograph, the obvious question pounding in his head: Where was she? And why did this feel like the beginning of something much larger? His hand hesitated over the doorframe, fingers tightening as he noticed a faint smell; something metallic, sharp, disturbing. Beneath the façade of suburban tranquility, a web of secrets had begun to tighten its grip around this seemingly ordinary neighborhood.

As days passed, the evidence piled up. The victim's friends and family refused to believe she had vanished voluntarily, and their stories wove into a pattern Julien couldn't ignore. There was an urgency to their eyes, a shared fear rooted in unspoken histories. Behind the scenes, whispers of old land disputes and familial betrayals surfaced through local contacts; all tangled in a web of greed and revenge spanning centuries. With each lead he followed, Julien felt the weight of unseen forces pressing down on him, building an oppressive pressure that threatened to drown him in the quiet town's tangled past.

Meanwhile, private thoughts swirled within Julien's mind. Memories of his own scars haunted him; mistakes made, friends lost, cases mishandled. He had come to believe that beneath every pristine surface, darkness lurks, waiting for the right moment to surface. Now, staring at the photograph again, he wondered if this case was a mirror of his own buried guilt; the lost trust, the family secrets kept hidden, the lies told to protect the innocent. Somewhere deep inside, a voice whispered that this wasn't just about a missing girl; it was about uncovering the long-overdue truth that someone wanted buried, safe and forgotten, but which now refused to stay silent.

Across town, in a dimly lit apartment, a figure stared at the same photograph on a small screen. Their breath was steady but deliberate, eyes flickering with a mixture of anger and purpose. This was no random disappearance. It was part of a pattern; victims chosen deliberately, each linked to unseen histories, to secrets held for generations. The killer, or perhaps the avenger, knew exactly what they were doing. They wanted something more than revenge; they sought to unearth truths that powerful forces had attempted to bury. Every step Julien took, every clue he uncovered, only drew him closer to the dark heart of this conspiracy. And that was a dangerous place to be.

The clock in the precinct ticked mercilessly, each second echoing louder in Julien's mind. As he sifted through old case files and personal histories, a name kept resurfacing; an ancestor intertwined with the land dispute that had once divided families across generations. This was no coincidence. A pattern was emerging, one that linked the past with the present in ways that made his skin crawl. Shadows stretched long and dark into his own life, threatening to envelope him entirely. He knew the killer was watching; calculating every move, eager to see if Julien would stumble in the darkness. The stakes kept rising, and with each passing hour, the boundary between justice and obsession blurred ever further.

That night, alone in his office, Julien found himself staring at a new cryptic message; the words scrawled hurriedly on a crumpled piece of paper left outside his door. It read:

"One more gone."

No signature, no warning, just those chilling words. His heart hammered against his ribs. He recognized the tone: personal, relentless, like a needle piercing through layers of deception. The message echoed in his mind as he realized the killer was not just targeting victims but was also trying to draw him into a game; one that threatened to unearth secrets better left buried. Julien's grip tightened on the worn edges of the paper, and he sensed that this was merely the beginning of the dominoes falling, each step pushing him deeper into a nightmare that linked the past with his own present fears.

Chapter 13

Cracks in the Facade

Jean-Luc sat hunched over his cluttered desk, the glow of his laptop casting long, flickering shadows across his face. His fingers hovered uncertainly over the keyboard, frustrated and exhausted. For days, he had been chasing clues; digital breadcrumbs and cryptic messages; that promised to unlock the mystery, but each lead seemed colder than the last. The missing files from his earlier inquiries, the ghostly gaps in the digital trail, gnawed at him like an irresolvable knot tightening with every passing hour.

He glanced around his sparse apartment, eyes darting over stacks of papers, folders, and half-eaten meals. The silence was oppressive, broken only by the occasional hum of the city beyond his window and the rhythmic tapping of his own heartbeat. His mind churned, trying to piece together why the digital clues had vanished, as if erased by some invisible hand. The more he pressed on, the clearer it became that someone; some sophisticated force; was deliberately obstructing him. The failure sharpened his frustration, simmering just beneath his skin, threatening to boil over at any moment.

In a rare burst of anger, Jean-Luc slammed his fist onto the desk, sending a pile of reports tumbling to the floor. "This isn't just bad luck," he muttered bitterly. "It's sabotage." His voice cracked, revealing the cracks in his own patience. It wasn't just about the case anymore; it was about the mounting sense that forces beyond his comprehension; or control; were actively working to keep him in the dark. Every dead-end made him question his instincts, his skills, and even his purpose. Frustration refused to let go, gnawing at his confidence like a dog with a bone he couldn't reach.

He reached for a cup of cold coffee, the bitter taste lingering on his tongue, mirroring his mood. His partner, Rousseau, had been more optimistic, always believing a breakthrough was possible. But Jean-Luc's mood had shifted from cautious hope to bleak suspicion. He stared at the screen, scrolling through lines of code that once seemed straightforward but now looked like the work of a master manipulator. It was as if the digital realm itself had conspired against him, deliberately concealing truths that could shatter everything he thought he knew. His frustration deepened, not just with the absence of clues but with himself; questioning whether he was missing something obvious or if he had been led astray from the start.

He remembered the moments when he had felt close; tiny sparks of hope flickering within the darkness. A strange, encrypted message that he'd deciphered only to find it was a red herring. An anonymous tip that proved to be a dead end. Each discovery, instead of bringing clarity, seemed to create another veil of confusion. It was a relentless maze where every turn only revealed more questions without answers. His fists clenched so tightly that his knuckles turned white, and for a second, he considered throwing the laptop across the room. That impulse was quickly smothered by a bitter realization: the more he fought, the more he was pushed back into the shadows.

In a quiet moment of desperation, Jean-Luc retrieved a small photograph from his wallet; one that featured Elise, innocent and smiling, before everything fell apart. The image reminded him of their last conversation, the promise to uncover the truth no matter what. Her face haunted him, fueling his anger and frustration. It wasn't just about the case anymore; it had become personal. Whoever was behind this digital maze knew him well, played with his mind, and pushed him to the edge. That feeling of helplessness cut deeper than any physical wound, stabbing at his resolve with every passing minute.

Suddenly, a strange noise interrupted his thoughts; an almost imperceptible shift in his apartment's silence. His instincts flared, every nerve awake and alert. Someone else was there, someone watching. His heart hammered wildly as he turned toward the door, every muscle tense. The air thickened with tension, a whisper of danger curling around him. The frustration, which had been simmering for days, burst forth in a rush of adrenaline. Every clue that had seemed out of reach now felt like a trap closing in. Jean-Luc's jaw clenched, frustration transforming into a primal focus. He knew this game was far bigger than he had imagined, and the next move would determine if he could break through the invisible barrier; or be consumed by it.

Chapter 14

The Legend Awakens

The air in the small village clung heavy with the scent of damp earth and fading leaves. Stones lined the narrow alleyways, whispering stories of centuries past, yet tonight, an insidious silence as thick as fog settled over its corners. It started with a simple discovery; the battered remnants of a crimson cloth caught tugging from beneath a loose brick in an abandoned cellar. Nobody immediately took notice, except for a handful of locals who muttered about strange happenings at night, shadows moving just beyond the reach of sight. For Marcus, a former investigator turned local historian, that fragment was a puzzle piece he hadn't asked for but was drawn to nonetheless; an echo of a legend long dismissed once the authorities deemed it folklore.

As dawn broke, Marcus returned to the cellar with a flashlight and that fragment of crimson fabric tightly clenched in his palm. The old stone walls seemed to breathe as if holding secrets meant to suffocate public memory. He brushed aside dust and grime, revealing a faint outline of what looked like a symbol; the unmistakable shape of a cross intertwined with a serpent, thin but deliberate, traced with deliberate care on the wall. His stomach clenched as memories surfaced; stories his grandfather used to whisper about a secret society called the *Homme Rouge*, a name loomed with dark shadows and dangerous truths buried beneath layers of history. But as he stared at the fresh blood-red stain smeared across the wall, a new realization seeped in; someone had been here recently, rewriting the story, perhaps even reenacting a long-forgotten ritual.

Across town, in a cramped apartment cluttered with books, folders, and half-scribbled notes, Elise's research suddenly flickered with new urgency. She had spent years chasing legends similar to the Homme Rouge, deciphering cryptic texts and deciphering symbols that haunted her dreams. Tonight, her phone buzzed; a single message encrypted in a strange, unfamiliar code. As she stared at it, her mind raced, connecting dots only she seemed to see. The message contained a black-and-white photograph, torn at the edges but unmistakably familiar. A group of figures gathered in the shadows, the same serpent-cross sym-bol subtly woven into their robes. It was the picture she'd seen in her grandfather's journal, suppressed for decades. But what truly made her heart pound was the faint, almost imperceptible handwriting scrawled across the bottom: "It's awakening again. The *Homme Rouge* must be stopped."

The quiet hum of the city was suddenly interrupted by a distant tapping; a sharp, deliberate sound that seemed to resonate from the very depths of her soul. Elise knew she wasn't alone; the shadows hiding in her apartment carried eyes that had been watching her for years, waiting for her to stumble across the truth. She tucked the photograph into her bag, her fingers trembling as she thought about the risks she faced. Whatever this meant, she was certain that someone or something wanted to keep the legend dormant, buried beneath centuries of lies and cover-ups. The line be-tween myth and reality blurred, and she felt the cold weight of history pressing heavily on her chest. Who-ever was on the other side of that message knew her name, and knew she had finally unmasked a truth that countless others had tried; and failed; to conceal.

Meanwhile, in a hidden chamber beneath the oldest part of the village, a figure cloaked in darkness knelt before a weathered altar. The air was thick with the scent of wax and forgotten memories. Without hesitation, the man reached beneath his heavy coat and pulled out a small, ornate box, ancient and covered with symbols eerily matching those in the cellar. His fingers traced the intricate carvings as a slow, sinister smile crept across his face. This was the moment he'd been waiting for; an awakening long prophesied by the founders of the *Homme Rouge*. The symbols on the box gleamed faintly in the dim light, and he whispered words from a language long abandoned. When he opened it, a faint pulse of crimson light spilled into the darkness, casting fleeting shadows across the walls. Inside lay a relic, a crimson talisman bound with old, uneven stitches; an artifact whispered to carry the essence of the ancient sect's most sacred; and most dangerous; power.

Back in the city's shadows, the pieces began to fall into place for Marcus and Elise, each unaware of the others' discoveries but instinctively pulled toward the same core truth. Rumors of missing persons, clandestine gatherings, and symbols etched into forgotten sites hinted at a larger, more malevolent force stirring beneath the surface. The legend of the *Homme Rouge* was no longer confined to dusty pages and whispered stories; it was stirring in the present, corrupting in ways that defied rational explanation. As they moved closer to the heart of the mystery, they had to confront the possibility that some forces; ancient, relentless; had never truly been dormant. They were reawakening, and with each new revelation, the danger grew exponentially, threatening to drag everything they loved into the shadow of the past. No one was safe, and in that darkness, secrets long buried threatened to explode with consequences that could change everything.

Chapter 15

The Web Tightens

The morning sun cast long shadows across the quiet suburban street, highlighting the unremarkable facade of the Johnson household. Inside, Emma Johnson hurriedly tossed some breakfast onto the table, her mind fractured into a thousand pieces by a restless night. Her husband, Mark, sat silently, gripping his coffee cup with knuckles white, as if anchoring himself to some fleeting hope. A small, folded piece of paper sat on the counter, its edges frayed from being handled repeatedly. She didn't notice it at first, lost in her thoughts about her missing sister, her desperation bubbling just beneath the surface. Yet, beneath that fragile veneer, Emma carried a secret; a silent plea she dared not voice; her sister's disappearance was no coincidence, and the truth was buried deeper than anyone suspected.

The day had begun with what seemed like a simple missing person report; her sister, Lisa, vanished without a trace a week ago from her apartment in the city. But Emma's gut had never accepted the ordinary explanation. She recalled the peculiar phone call she overheard last night, a murmur of voices that weren't supposed to be there. She had been in her room, windows open to the warm breeze, when she noticed a voice whispering from the other side of the wall. Faint but distinct, it had said, "The truth will come out. We're watching you." Emma had no idea who was listening, but the message had frozen her blood. Now, clutching the paper, she wondered if her sister's disappearance was part of some bigger, uglier scheme; something cunningly hidden behind the veneer of peaceful suburbia.

Across town, in a dimly lit office cluttered with papers and old files, Detective Jean-Luc Rousseau stared at the photographs before him. A series of images; grainy, yet disturbingly familiar; showed locations linked to the victims' last known movements. Each scene was eerily similar: abandoned buildings, a single symbol scrawled hastily on the wall; an angular, sinister sigil that seemed to repeat across the city's darker corners. Rousseau's brow furrowed as he traced the connection to a decades-old case involving a clandestine society tied to local elites. The patterns whispered of something ancient and deadly. His instincts told him that the case was more than a string of murders; it was a thread unraveling a web of corruption woven into the fabric of the city itself. Somewhere within these tangled layers lay a lie so deeply buried that only relentless pursuit could unearth it.

Back in the shadows of that suburban house, Emma's phone vibrated abruptly, jolting her from her thoughts. She hesitated, then answered with trembling fingers. On the other end, a voice; strained, hurried; said:

"You don't know who I am, but I've seen what's happening. They're watching, and Lisa's in danger. You need to find the truth before it's too late."

The line went dead, leaving Emma gasping, clutching the device as if it could offer her some clarity. Her pulse raced, nerves fraying with each passing second. Who was this mysterious caller? Friend or foe? Did they truly hold the key to her sister's whereabouts, or was this another trap? Every instinct told her to run, to escape the shadows creeping into her life. Yet, deep down, she knew she had no choice but to confront whatever darkness lurked behind the smooth surface of her quiet neighborhood.

Meanwhile, Jean-Luc examined a discarded item found at one of the crime scenes; an old, tarnished locket engraved with the same symbol seen on the walls. Inside, a faded photograph showed a group of figures from decades past, including a face that seemed disturbingly familiar: a scarred man whose eyes held the promise of secrets long buried. Rousseau's fingers instinctively clenched around the object, feeling the weight of history pressing down on him. How did this relic connect to the current murders? Could it be a clue left intentionally, a taunt from whoever was orchestrating all of this? His mind spun with the possibilities, each one darker than the last. Somewhere out there, a hidden truth lingered; something that threatened to shatter the fragile peace of their lives and reveal that the sins of the past had never truly been buried.

As the hours passed, Emma found herself drawn into a clandestine world of whispers and half-truths. Her late-night research led her to old news articles about the city's founding families, revealing a tangled history of land disputes, greed, and cover-ups. Her finger traced the line of a map; marked with crosses and circles; highlighting properties that had vanished from official records. The revelation haunted her: her family's ancestors had been embroiled in a land dispute with an influential council member whose name kept recurring in dark whispers. Every piece of information added weight to her suspicion that her sister's disappearance might be connected to her family's buried secrets. With each new discovery, the walls of her reality crumbled further, exposing layers of corruption and ancient vendettas that refused to stay buried. She knew that by seeking the truth, she was treading on dangerous ground; but her desperation over Lisa's fate propelled her forward.

In the depths of the city's archaic underground tunnels, Rousseau and his team moved cautiously, flashlights slicing through the darkness. They navigated narrow, cobweb-laden passages that seemed to stretch forever beneath the historic sites. Every step echoed with the weight of history's silence, and the air grew colder, heavier. Rousseau's mind kept coming back to the symbols carved into the walls; fanglike shapes that seemed to watch him as he advanced. Here, beneath the city's surface, old secrets and newer shadows converged. Somewhere in these hidden depths, the killer had left another message; perhaps the final piece of the puzzle. Rousseau's gut warned him that beyond these tunnels lay the truth, but also that the threat had followed them underground. Tension built palpably in the silence, each discovery bringing them closer to a revelation that could unravel all they had uncovered so far; and perhaps, in the process, unearth a final, deadly revelation that none of them were ready for.

Chapter 16

The Labyrinth of Paris

The labyrinth beneath Paris was not the kind the tourists marveled at when they whispered about the catacombs. It's a network of forgotten tunnels, sealed passages, and crumbling stone corridors that seemed more alive than inert. Dubois studied the map on his phone, fingers tracing the faint outlines of old sewer routes that had long since fallen out of official use. His heart pounded with a strange mix of anticipation and unease; he could almost hear the muffled echoes of footsteps from years past, ghosts of those who had vanished into the darkness and never returned. Standing at the entrance, he took a shaky breath, knowing that in these shadows, the killer had left more than just clues; he had taunted them with a twisted sense of control. This was no ordinary hideout; it was a battle-ground for a deadly game of wit and will, where every turn could be a trap or a breakthrough.

As Dubois and Rousseau descended into the depths, the air grew thick and cold, carrying the scent of damp stone and something far more ominous; an echo of betrayal. The killer's messages had begun surfacing in unexpected places: cryptic symbols sketched in decades-old graffiti, seemingly random snippets of secret code whispered through whispers in the wind. Rousseau eyed the dark corners alertly, clutching her flashlight tighter.

"He's playing with us," she muttered, her voice echoing strangely in the confined space. "This is more than just revenge. It's strategic; something personal, yet rooted in ancient grievances."

Dubois nodded, feeling the weight of the history they were uncovering. Victims' names from years past flickered through his mind like ghosts, all connected to the underground, connected to those legends of the vengeful *Homme Rouge*; the Red Man; whose legend haunted these tunnels, whispering promises of retribution for past betrayals.

They reached a narrow passage, the ceiling dangerously low and the footing uneven. Rousseau's eyes flickered to a fragment of rusted metal wedged in the wall, a seemingly insignificant detail that hinted at previous human presence. As they pressed forward, a sudden noise made Rousseau freeze; faint but unmistakable, like the scraping of nails on stone. Instinctively, Dubois raised his weapon, heart pounding in his chest. He knew their predator was nearby, watching, waiting for the perfect moment to strike. Every shadow seemed to hide a secret, every sound amplified and distorted in the darkness. Somewhere ahead, the killer was with them; a ghost lurking just beyond the edge of sight. The tension grew unbearable, each step bringing them closer to the truth but also deeper into the trap.

Then came the message; scrawled carefully on a disused brick wall, barely visible but unmistakable once seen: a phrase in ancient French that spoke of betrayal and revenge. Dubois studied it, feeling a chill crawl along his spine. It was a message meant for him, meant to provoke, to remind him of his own past, of the lines he dared not cross. The killer's voice; silent but loud; resonated in his mind: "We are not so different, you and I. We both seek justice, but I know the way you think. I've studied you. And now, I want to see how far you're willing to go."

The words lingered, echoing in the hollow space as if daring him to follow the trail deeper into the darkness. Behind him, Rousseau kept her composure, but her eyes betrayed her weariness. She knew this was a game, a dangerous chess match, where every move could seal their fate or bring them closer to the truth that had been buried for centuries.

Suddenly, a faint flicker of light appeared in the distance; dim and irregular, like a heartbeat beneath the rubble. Dubois gestured for silence, and they advanced cautiously, every sense heightened. As they drew nearer, the outline of a small chamber revealed itself, haphazardly sealed with old planks and tied with rusty wire. Inside, the flickering light revealed a figure; a silhouette hunched over a table cluttered with papers, photographs, and symbols. It was the killer, waiting for them. Time seemed to stretch as Dubois and Rousseau entered the space; a carefully orchestrated trap designed to taunt them, to pit their knowledge against a mind as sharp as their own. The killer looked up slowly, a predatory smile curling on his lips, eyes glittering with a cold, calculated fury. This was more than a chase now; it was a final confrontation; the moment where truth, vengeance, and death collided.

Chapter 17

Shadows of Elise

The first time Detective Marc Rousseau saw Elise's photograph, it had been tucked into a neglected corner of his desk; almost like an afterthought. It was a grainy black-and-white shot, faded at the edges, showing a young woman with sharp eyes and an uncertain smile standing beside an ornate iron gate. She looked out of place in the hurried snapshot, her gaze fixed just past the camera, as if she sensed the danger creeping behind her. He didn't remember where he'd found it, but the image had haunted him ever since, whispering unspoken stories that refused to stay buried. It struck him as eerily similar to the missing person reports he'd reviewed; yet also disturbingly different, as if it hinted at something deeper, darker than he could comprehend at first glance.

Outside his office window, the city slept under a heavy, clouded sky. Shadows stretched long across quiet suburban streets, dimly lit by flickering lanterns and distant car alarms. It was an ordinary neighborhood, the kind where secrets were buried beneath manicured lawns and peeling porch paint. Yet, within those seemingly placid horizons, Rousseau felt the weight of a storm approaching. He could sense that the faint hum of ordinary life was hiding something more sinister, something that connected his current investigation to a past he'd tried to forget. The photograph was just the beginning, a key to a door he didn't realize he was approaching, each step slowly tightening around him.

His partner, Rousseau's old confidant Jean-Luc Dubois, had come by earlier with a nervous look, eyeing the photo as if it might reveal a terrible truth.

"That girl looks familiar," Jean-Luc murmured, tracing patterns in the faded grain. "Have you checked her against the missing persons reports from twenty years ago? The ones I've been digging into?"

Rousseau nodded slowly, feeling a dull ache behind his temples. There was no easy answer; only a thousand questions spiraling out of control: Why did her eyes strike such a chord? Was she linked to the recent victims, or just another ghost from a past that refused to stay silent? The similarities were undeniable, yet everything about their stories seemed carefully woven to remain hidden beneath layers of illusion and lies.

Later that night, as Rousseau sifted through more photographs, documents, and reports in his cluttered apartment, a strange sense of familiarity settled over him. His research had led to the discovery of a pattern; one that linked the current disappearances with a series of crimes that went back decades, buried beneath the layers of official history. There was a recurring figure, often hiding in the background of old court records, mysterious insignias etched into clandestine documents, symbols that resonated with the one in Elise's photograph. The weight of it pressed heavily on him, like a shadow sliding insidiously across his mind, threatening to engulf him. The threads tied to Elise's photo wove into an unseen net, tightening the stakes, reminding him that this was no ordinary case. It was a mirror to something he'd long tried to forget; an unsettling parallel that refused to remain in the past.

The more Rousseau uncovered, the more visceral the connection felt. One photograph in particular haunted him; a picture from an archive he'd risked digging through late into the night. It depicted the same iron gate, aged and rusted, with another young woman standing behind it, her back turned, partially obscured by shadows. Her posture betrayed fear, yet her eyes, bright and searching, seemed to plead for help. Every detail echoed Elise's old research, which had once seemed like an academic exercise but now revealed itself as a warning. Someone had been watching, or worse, orchestrating. The implication was darker still; who was orchestrating the pattern of disappearances? Who was pulling the strings behind the scenes, and how deep did this web of deceit go? As Rousseau's mind raced, an icy chill spread through him, blurring the line between past and present, unmaking the thin veneer of reality.

In the obscure hours of the night, that unsettling feeling grew stronger. Rousseau's apartment, usually a sanctuary of order, felt suffocating. Every creak of the building sounded like an ominous whisper, urging him to look beneath the surface. His thoughts fixated on Elise's unreadable smile; her eyes, windows into a world of secrets; and the strange parallels to the current victims. They all seemed connected, not just by circumstance but by an unspoken compulsion, as if some unseen force was guiding the pattern. Somewhere in the depths of his mind, a faint memory flickered: Elise's research, her obsession with a shadowy figure known as the *Homme Rouge*, and the mysterious symbol she'd uncovered. Those memories felt like threads pulling him deeper, revealing that the past wasn't dead. It lurked just beneath the surface; waiting to collapse everything he thought he knew.

As dawn broke over the city, Rousseau sat at his worn desk, eyes scanning the latest batch of photographs; a ritual he knew all too well. Time had blurred the edges, distorting images, but the unease remained sharp and clear. The pattern was becoming undeniable. The victims, Elise, the mysterious symbol; each was a piece of a puzzle already assembled, waiting for him to connect the final corners. The resemblance of the young women in the photos to Elise's image grew impossible to ignore. Somehow, they were echoes; reflections of the same unresolved trauma, the same dark secret, repeating across time. The idea that someone was deliberately recreating history; either to punish, to hide, or perhaps to reenact some twisted version of justice; made his stomach churn. The parallels weren't just disturbing; they were relentless, and Rousseau knew that confronting them would mean facing not just a killer, but a deeper, more sinister conspiracy lurking in the shadows, weaving its silent threads through everything.

… Chapter 18

The Family's Secret

The grand mansion loomed atop the hill like a silent sentinel, its windows dark and uninviting against the faint glow of dawn. Inside, shadows clung tightly to the ancient furniture, and a heavy silence pervaded the air, broken only by the distant muffled sounds of life beyond its walls. For years, this house had been the seat of authority in the town; an enduring symbol of wealth, influence, and unspoken secrets. The man who held sway over its corridors, Vincennes Moreau, was no longer seen often outside; his presence was felt more in whispers and sidelong glances, the kind that carried weight and obligation.

Vincennes was a man in his late sixties, still upright despite the visible wear on his face, his silver hair meticulously combed back, as if brushing away years of conflict. He was a figure others deferred to without question, a patriarch whose influence seeped into every corner of the community. Behind the polished veneer, however, lurked a mind sharp with cunning and an unyielding determination to maintain the family's dominance. Every handshake, every carefully worded conversation was a chess move in a game that had played out for decades, where the stakes were not just money, but control over the land, history, and legacy itself.

As the morning sun cast a muted light through the heavy curtains, Vincennes sat at his grand desk, a glass of dark Bordeaux in hand. His eyes, cold and assessing, lingered on a faded photograph; an image from long ago, showing himself alongside his father and grandfather, all dressed in suits and stiff smiles. This photograph was more than just a keepsake; it was a reminder of the unbreakable chain of authority stretching back generations. His succession was never in doubt, partly because the family's power was entrenched in systems of corruption, partly because of his ruthless grip on the family's secrets. For Vincennes, his word was law, and that law extended to the smallest details of the town's affairs.

Just as he was about to pour himself another glass, a sharply dressed aide entered with a hurried knock. Quietly, the man handed Vincennes a sealed envelope, whose edges bore the faded insignia of an old family crest; a relic of a time when land, bloodlines, and loyalty defined one's worth. Vincennes's gaze hardened as he broke the seal and unfolded the letter. It was a warning, veiled in formal language, hinting at unrest within the family; an outsider's concern about recent disclosures, whispers that threatened to expose the cracks beneath the polished surface. That outsider was no stranger; she had a name that struck a nerve within him; Elise Laurent; a woman whose past investigations had already cast shadows over the family's reputation.

He handed the letter back to his aide with a curt nod, the faint hiss of the paper crackling the only sound as he processed its implications. Vincennes had always been a master at control, wielding influence like a weapon that cut both ways. To him, secrets were currency, and the more you kept locked away, the stronger your position. But mistakes had a way of surfacing; small leaks, unnoticed cracks; each one capable of unleashing a tide that could drown everything he had built. His mind quickly shifted, calculating the next move, knowing that power came with risks, but also knowing that retreat was never an option when your entire family's legacy was at stake.

The quiet around him thickened as memories of old alliances, betrayals, and sacrifices played out in his mind. He had known that the land they clung to represented more than ownership; it symbolized dominance, history, and vengeance. The family's influence was rooted in a web of deals and cover-ups, each link reinforced by intimidation and silence. Vincennes had long since mastered the art of silence; a skill that kept his enemies guessing and his allies loyal. But beneath that calm exterior simmered a growing suspicion; someone was probing too deep, and he would need to act before the cracks in his empire widened beyond repair.

Down the hall, hidden behind door after door, children and relatives moved cautiously, unaware of how tightly their patriarch's grip extended into every aspect of their lives. Vincennes's son, Philippe, was outside the house now, meeting with a trusted business partner, carefully discussing plans that would further cement the family's control over local enterprises. Every word was measured, every gesture calculated. The power Vincennes wielded was not just born from wealth, but from the subtle manipulation of systems; local courts, law enforcement, even media outlets; each one a pawn in his grand game. The family's reputation was a fortress, built stone by stone over generations, and Vincennes's decisions today would determine how many more years it would stand tall.

His thoughts were interrupted by a soft knock at the door as his granddaughter, Isabelle, entered quietly. The young woman's eyes flicked with unease, her face betraying a depth of awareness far beyond her years. She hesitated before speaking in a hushed voice, mentioning her concerns about the increasingly aggressive inquiries into the family's past; about the land disputes, about documents she'd seen that hinted at something more sinister buried beneath their history. Vincennes's smile remained cold, a mask forged by decades of discipline. He nodded slowly, his mind already racing through possible responses. This was not the first threat to his authority, and certainly not the last, but the stakes had never been higher.

In that moment, Vincennes realized that the silence surrounding his family's legacy was about to be shattered, and the foundation of his power; so painstakingly maintained; might soon be tested by truths long suppressed. He poured himself another glass, the dark liquid catching the dim light, and took a long, measured sip. His eyes fixed on the horizon, darkening with resolve. There were secrets buried in this family's past, secrets that could topple his reign if revealed. And he would do whatever it took to keep them hidden; because, for him, the true strength of a patriarch lay not just in wealth or influence, but in the unyielding control over the stories others dared not uncover.

Chapter 19

False Trails and Buried Truths

The dim glow of the streetlamp cast a flickering amber light over the quiet suburb, where the mere mention of a missing person had initially seemed like an ordinary concern. Emma had always been a model neighbor; quiet, unassuming, with her yard meticulously cared for. But last night, when her husband found the basement door slightly ajar and the kitchen's faint scent of burnt coffee lingering in the air, a strange unease started to simmer beneath the surface of their peaceful neighborhood. No signs of struggle, no frantic calls for help; just that odd, wilting smell and the faintest trail of muddy footprints leading to the backyard's dense hedge. It was enough to unsettle anyone, yet most dismissed it as a minor quarrel or perhaps an accidental departure.

As Detective Marc Rousseau arrived at the scene in the early morning haze, he noticed the faint outlines of footprints leading from the backyard to the street, but they seemed deliberately vague, as if someone had tried to erase their steps. The fact that Emma's disappearance seemed so quiet, almost understated, didn't sit right with him. He spoke briefly with her husband, who looked exhausted, eyes hollow, lips pressed tight as if fighting back a story he didn't want to tell. Rousseau sensed the layers beneath this simple case; something more sinister lurking just beneath. It was here, amid the mundane suburban facades, that the killer's deception had begun, cloaking their motives in ordinary appearances while hiding a chilling, calculated intent.

Rousseau's instinct told him to dig deeper, to question not just the facts but the narrative surrounding Emma's life. He sifted through her belongings, discovering a stack of old photographs tucked away in a dusty shoebox. One picture caught his eye; a faded image from years ago, showing Emma standing beside an older man with a stern face. Beneath the photo, a scribbled note read: "They're watching." The cryptic message sent a shiver through him. Someone had been watching Emma long before her disappearance, manipulating her environment without her knowledge. This was no run-of-the-mill abduction. It was a game crafted by a mind skilled at deception, someone who thrived on misdirection. Rousseau knew that to catch the killer, he had to understand that deception; the layers of lies carefully woven to hide the truth; had already been set in motion.

Chapter 20

The Cryptic Invitation

The wind had a sharp bite that evening, tugging at the edges of the small, cluttered apartment where Dubois sat alone, a pile of unopened mail forgotten on the table beside his worn leather chair. The soft hum of the city lingered outside; car horns, distant sirens, footsteps on damp pavement; but inside, he felt the silence pressing in like a weight pulling him down. Among the jumble of papers and faded photographs spread across the table, one kept drawing his attention; a small, folded note with a single word scrawled in hurried handwriting: *Find.* No signature, no indication of origin, just that: *Find.* It had arrived earlier that morning, slipped under his door without fanfare, its message clear but cryptic, a challenge he couldn't ignore.

He had been chasing shadows for weeks now, unraveling clues that refused to align neatly. A missing person here, an overheard whisper there, an old photograph of a man in a muddled crowd; all pieces that seemed disconnected yet somehow purposeful. Each step further into this puzzle revealed a tangled history stretching back centuries, buried beneath layers of silence and complicity. And yet, tonight, the stakes felt higher than ever. The voice on the note; implied not just a plea for discovery but a warning; had pierced his defenses, stirring something dark and unfamiliar within him. His instincts, hardened over years of hard cases, told him this was no random joke. Someone knew he was close, and that person had crossed a line.

Sitting back, Dubois reached for the glass of whisky he often kept nearby, the amber liquid catching the dim light and shimmering for a moment. He hesitated, then took a small sip, feeling the burn settle deep into his chest. The quieting of his thoughts was short-lived; his phone buzzed suddenly, jolting him from his reverie. The screen flashed a new message, this time from an unknown number: You're getting too close. Stop digging. A cold shiver ran down his spine; not because of the threat but because he recognized the handwriting, frantic and uneven, the same as the notes he'd studied from old files. Whoever was behind this knew him better than he liked. They knew what he'd uncovered, and most ominously, what he intended to uncover next.

On impulse, he reached into a drawer and pulled out a faded leather-bound notebook; the same one Elise had left behind, filled with scribbles, maps, and coded symbols that seemed to echo from another lifetime. Her research had always straddled the line between obsession and insight; now, that line was blurring ominously. As his fingers traced her handwriting, a fleeting image flickered in his mind; her face, the expression of fierce determination carved into her features. Elise had been onto something, something larger than her own disappearance. He remembered how she'd warned him about secrets buried beneath history's veneer; secrets some would kill to keep hidden. Now, with the note pressing in, it seemed her warning was more urgent than ever.

The door suddenly creaked open behind him, causing him to jolt upright. A figure stood silhouetted in the doorway, hesitant, tense. Dubois recognized Rousseau's silhouette; a breath of relief fluttered briefly in his chest. Rousseau stepped inside, clutching an envelope thick with notes and photographs; evidence they'd collected together over the last few days. His face was grim, eyes dark with exhaustion.

"You got the message too? This isn't random. Someone's playing with us," Rousseau said, voice hushed but insistent.

Dubois nodded, placing the note back on the table with care.

"Whatever this is, it's personal. Someone knows who we are; and what we're after."

His voice was low, but there was a steel edge beneath it, a resolve forged through countless nights in pursuit of justice. They exchanged a glance; partners bound by a shared purpose, yet painfully aware that every new clue pulled them deeper into the shadows.

Their shared concern deepened with each passing moment. Below their feet, the city pulsed with its endless rhythm, oblivious to their mounting danger. Outside, a figure in a dark coat lurked in the alley, eyes fixed on the apartment building; watching, waiting. Inside, they knew the danger was closer than ever. A series of symbols and dates scribbled in Elise's journal came rushing back to Dubois's mind, hinting at a conspiracy that reached far beyond petty crimes and into the heart of powerful institutions. Someone had gone to great lengths to erase history, and now, that history was fighting back. His determination intensified. If he didn't act tonight, the next victim might be closer than ever; or maybe, already, it was too late.

He looked sharply at Rousseau.

"We have to move faster. Whoever sent that note knows our next target."

Rousseau nodded, pulling out a small laminated map marked with red crosses and cryptic annotations. Shadows danced across the walls as they pinned down their next move, minds racing against the ticking clock. The notes, the photographs, the anonymous threats;

they all pointed toward something buried deep beneath the city's surface, a secret that had been kept
hidden for generations. A secret that, if revealed, could
upheave everything they thought they understood
about their past; and their present. As they prepared to
leave, Dubois cast one last glance at the note, its single
word echoing ominously in his mind: *Find.*

Chapter 21

Beneath the Palace

The cold air beneath the Louvre was thick with silence, disturbed only by the faint drip of water echoing through narrow corridors. The team moved cautiously, their footsteps muted against the ancient stones, each step resonating with the weight of centuries buried beneath their feet. Claude Rousseau's flashlight cut a narrow beam ahead, illuminating faded murals and crumbling brickwork that seemed to pulse with a quiet, haunting life of their own. To the untrained eye, this might have looked like just another underground tunnel system, but to those who knew the city's shadowed history, it was a network veiled in secrets; hidden passages carved for purposes long forgotten, now holding the key to unraveling the killer's madness.

The air grew denser as they pressed forward, the walls closing in like an embrace from the past. Dubois kept his gun drawn, eyes sharp and ears attuned to every sound; a scratch, a whisper, the faint scrape of something unseen gliding just beyond their sight. In this darkness, their flashlights barely reached past the edges of ancient bricks, revealing glimpses of what once might have been a grand hall or a chamber, now succumbed to decay. Elise's research had spoken of these tunnels; vast, labyrinthine routes beneath the city that had served as escape routes, hiding places, or clandestine meeting spots for those seeking refuge from an increasingly hostile world. Now, it was eerily quiet, yet thick with the presence of something sinister; something that had been waiting in the shadows for centuries.

The team paused at a junction where recent disturbances had gouged a jagged entrance into the wall. Rousseau knelt, brushing aside loose debris to reveal faint symbols scrawled on the stone; marks that somehow resonated with the ritualistic symbols found at previous crime scenes. Dubois studied them intently, his mind racing through the possible connections. The killer's pattern was unmistakable: each victim, each location, seemed tied to this underground web. As they advanced further, they noticed a faint draft seeping through a narrow crawlspace, the air carrying a faint scent; something metallic, dusty, and old. Behind a loose panel, they discovered a hollow space, just large enough to crawl through, leading into an almost oubliette of forgotten corridors and hidden chambers. It was here that all the clues converged, where the darkness beneath the city seemed to whisper warnings and secrets alike.

Suddenly, Rousseau froze, voice hushed but tense.

"Look at this," he said, pointing to a small niche partially concealed behind a collapsed wall.

Inside, shards of broken pottery and an array of old, tarnished coins suggested someone had lived or hidden here long ago. Dubois examined the relics carefully, feeling the weight of history pressing against him. It was evident this wasn't just an abandoned tunnel; this was a deliberate hiding spot, used over the years for purposes lost to time. As they moved on, they began to see evidence of recent activity; a discarded cloth, fresh footprints in the dust, and a faint trail of smeared grease leading deeper into the darkness. The killer was here, somewhere ahead, orchestrating their next move, their presence more tangible than ever as the shadows grew thicker and the air colder around them.

Deeper still, the corridors widened into a room the size of a small chapel. Broken statues and decrepit votive offerings littered the floor, remnants of old rituals performed in centuries past. It was here that Dubois caught a glimpse of something startling; an untouched notebook, its pages filled with handwritten notes in a hurried, trembling hand. As he flipped through the pages, a chill crawled up his spine. The entries spoke of revenge, of betrayal, and of a relentless pursuit of justice rooted not in law but in personal vengeance. Each word seemed to echo with a madness that reflected the killer's own fractured psyche.

Suddenly, a faint noise drew their attention; a soft scraping, like fingernails against stone, came from the darkness beyond. The passage was alive with unseen sentience, and they knew that whatever had been lurking in these shadows was now aware of their presence. Every instinct urged them to move fast, to escape this enshrouded nightmare, but they also understood that the heart of the killer's twisted sanctuary lay just ahead, waiting, perhaps, for the ultimate confrontation.

Chapter 22

The Unmasking

The room was cloaked in shadow, the faint glow of streetlights slipping through a narrow slit in the heavy curtains. Dubois moved quietly, almost instinctively, knowing that whatever awaited him in that abandoned warehouse could shatter everything he thought he knew. His heart hammered in his chest; not from fear, but from a growing sense of dread that this was no ordinary confrontation. The air was thick with dust and a faint scent of mold, reminding him that the place hadn't seen daylight in years, yet tonight, it held a secret that would alter his course forever.

Across the narrow room, the killer; an obsessed scholar and a relic of past betrayals; waited, their presence felt more than seen. The man's eyes flickered with a strange mixture of calm and menace, like someone who'd long ago abandoned the notion of mercy. Chains of old books and tattered papers cluttered nearby, evidence of endless research into dangerous lore and forbidden histories. It was clear this wasn't just a murderer haunted by impulse, but a master of manipulation, driven by a twisted sense of justice rooted deep in centuries of injustice and family vengeance.

Dubois knew this moment had been building for years, buried beneath layers of hidden truths and half-forgotten betrayals. His mind flashed back to Elise, whose research had unwittingly uncovered the strongest link to this man; and to a darker world that refused to stay buried. As he took a cautious step forward, his entire body tensed, aware that the final confrontation was at hand. The killer's motives ran much deeper than personal madness; they were intertwined with a legacy of land theft, corrupt power, and centuries-old grievances that refused to die quietly.

The silence was thick but thickened further when the killer finally spoke, voice low and deliberate.

"You think you understand justice, Dubois? This isn't about law or morals. It's about restoring what was stolen; what they thought they could hide forever."

The words hung in the air, echoing like a curse, as clues and memories clicked into place in Dubois's mind. Every clue, every dead end, all pointing to a conspiracy much larger than he had imagined; one in which Elise's research and his family's dark past formed critical pieces of a puzzle someone desperately wanted to keep sealed.

He took another step, the crack of his boot breaking a moment of tense stillness. His hand hovered near his weapon, but he knew that the true battle couldn't be fought with guns alone. This man had spent years mastering secrecy, weaving stories to mask his true intent. Dubois realized that beating him meant unraveling not just the physical trap, but the tangled web of history and vengeance that had fueled this long-running cycle. Somewhere in the shadows, the killer's eyes flickered again, as if daring him to come closer, daring him to uncover the truth that had remained buried for so long.

The killer revealed a battered journal, filled with torn pages, scribbled notes, and an ominous symbol etched repeatedly in dark ink.

"You dig through the past, you will find the roots of all this," he whispered, voice thick with venom. "And when you do, you'll see that some debts aren't meant to be paid; they're meant to be avenged."

Dubois felt his stomach tighten, realizing that this was more than just a murder case. It was a personal crusade rooted in bloodlines, betrayal, and justice twisted beyond recognition. Watching the man's steady gaze, he knew this final encounter would test everything; trust, morality, even his own resolve.

Chapter 23

Forgetting Is Not Allowed

The air felt heavy, almost suffocating, as the dim glow of a flickering candle cast uneven shadows across the cramped chamber. Dubois moved cautiously, muscles tense, every step echoing softly against the cold stone walls. He knew he wasn't alone; this place had been designed to hide secrets, and those secrets had a way of sticking around, even when the lights were out. His eyes darted around the room, searching for any sign of the killer or clues that might explain why Elise's missing research and the cryptic symbols found at the crime scene were woven into a tapestry of centuries-old resentment. The silence pressed down harder with every passing second, punctuated only by the faint scrape of a loose stone shifting beneath his foot.

Across from him, the figure lurked in the shadows; calm, almost resigned, yet undeniably dangerous. The killer's breath was rapid but controlled, eyes flickering beneath the hood of a dark cloak that dragged slightly on the cold floor. It was a game of nerves now, a tense exchange of gazes that stretched into eternity. Their history rippled beneath the surface; both knew these kinds of confrontations were rarely about mere vengeance anymore. Here, old grudges; buried beneath layers of time; had clawed their way back to life, threatening to explode at any moment. The killer's lips curled into a faint, unsettling smile as if they relished the duality of power and vulnerability in this dark dance.

Suddenly, the flickering candle sputtered, its small flame shrinking to a stub before dying out completely, plunging them into stifling darkness. A sharp click echoed through the silence; an unmistakable sound of a trigger being pulled, and Dubois felt his pulse leap. In the pitch-black gloom, he could hear the faint shuffling of movement, a person approaching, slow and deliberate. The killer's voice whispering in the darkness, low and menacing: "You think you're closing in? You have no idea what you're about to wake up."

Every nerve in Dubois tensed as he reached instinctively for his weapon, feeling the cold handle of the pistol in his palm, fingers trembling slightly. The unseen threat pressed closer, and he knew that whatever was about to unfold would change everything he believed; about the case, about Elise, and about himself.

Then, a whisper, nearly inaudible, sliced through the space.

"You've come too far to walk away now," it hissed.

Shadows shifted on the walls as the killer stepped into a faint crack of moonlight sneaking in through an unseen gap, revealing just enough of their face; pale, scarred, haunted. A face that had seen too much but hadn't yet been broken. The silence that followed felt like a living thing, waiting for the next move. Dubois's mind raced through the puzzle pieces: betrayal, family vengeance, long-buried secrets buried beneath layers of history that had festered beneath the surface for generations. The shadows seemed to pulse with a life of their own, as if trying to swallow the truth whole, holding its secrets tight until someone brave; or desperate; came to pry them loose.

"Why are you doing this?" Dubois finally forced out, voice steady but strained.

The killer's eyes narrowed, revealing hints of desperation beneath their calm exterior.

"Because history forgets," they said softly, voice gravelly. "And those who forget are doomed to relive it. Elise uncovered too much; she was close to unveiling what some wanted buried forever. I can't let that happen again."

At that moment, the killer's hand shot forward, a glint catching the dying moonlight; a knife, now pressed against Dubois's chest. The world seemed to stand still as it was all too real: a choice, a confrontation, a final resistance. This was more than a hunt; it was a reckoning rooted in blood and betrayal that stretched back centuries. The shadows waited in silence, holding the crucial truths that everyone else had long since turned away from, ready to swallow the truth or reveal it in a final, deadly act.

Breathing deeply, Dubois felt the weight of history pressing down on his shoulders, pounding in his ears. His mind raced to Elise's research, her relentless pursuit of justice, and how it had led her into this dark abyss. The killer's grip tightened, ready to strike, but Dubois steadied himself, eyes locked onto the scarred face before him. Whatever secrets this chamber hid, whatever lies had been kept for generations, he was determined to uncover them; before it was too late. The shadows stretched and flickered again as the killer's voice broke the tense silence with a murderously calm warning:

"When darkness falls, truths are revealed. But not everyone survives to see the light."

In that instant, as the two faces inched closer, a faint, distant clatter echoed from the corridor outside; an ominous reminder that their fight was far from over, and that perhaps, this was only the beginning of something far worse.

Chapter 24

Echoes of Justice

The small town of Saint-Jean's Banks was an unlikely place for darkness to thrive beneath its sleepy streets and manicured lawns. On the surface, it was a quiet suburb, where mothers pushed strollers along tree-lined avenues and neighbors exchanged smiles over picket fences. But behind closed doors, secrets festered like wounds nobody dared to tend. That morning, Grace Turner slid her key into the lock of her seldom-used backyard shed, expecting nothing more than a routine clean-up. Instead, her breath hitched, her fingers curling around an object that shouldn't have belonged there; an old, faded photograph, partially buried beneath a pile of rusted tools and torn canvases. The image shimmered in the weak sunlight, revealing a distorted face; eyes hollow and lips bloody; staring back at her from a forgotten past she had thought long buried.

Grace's heart hammered as a flood of memories surged. That face was her brother Tommy, last seen nineteen years ago amid whispers of a family scandal, lost to the shadows of a unresolved police case. Her knees buckled and she sank onto the cracked concrete, clutching the photograph as if holding onto a dying thread of hope. She knew she wasn't imagining it. This was the same boy she'd tracked through old photo albums, the one who vanished without explanation after the night the family's dark history came crashing down. Her mind raced; how had this photograph ended up here, and what did it mean? Rumors of betrayal, a cover-up involving powerful figures, and her own unyielding suspicion that her brother's disappearance wasn't accidental; the weight sank heavily on her chest.

Meanwhile, far beneath the glittering surface of Paris's historic heart, Jean-Luc Dubois sat hunched over a cluttered desk in his dimly lit apartment. The case that had haunted him for years pulsed like a wound he refused to let close. His latest breakthrough had been a whisper; a fragile thread connecting the recent murders to a clandestine society rooted in centuries-old grievances. Every clue felt like slipping sand, deliberately placed falsehoods designed to mislead. He ran his fingers through his hair, the scent of stale coffee mingling with the smoke billowing out of his cigarette. Somewhere in the shadows, unseen eyes observed him, waiting for him to stumble into the trap.

Dubois knew the killer was baiting him, but he also believed the trail would lead him straight into the heart of a conspiracy that linked the past to the present in a fateful web of vengeance, secrets long buried beneath Paris's storied streets.

Back in Saint-Jean's Banks, Grace's discovery was just the beginning. She couldn't ignore the parallels; an unspoken history woven through her family, betrayal lurking in old land deeds, stories dismissed as folklore. The photograph seemed to pulse with life, as if it carried a message only she could decipher. The more she examined it, the clearer it became: this was a warning, or perhaps an invitation. Her phone buzzed beside her as a message appeared from an unknown number; coded, cryptic, daring her to confront what lay beneath the surface. The sender hinted at a truth buried deep within her lineage, a secret that threatened to undo everything she'd ever known. Fear and determination fought inside her, a reminder that some debts could never be forgiven, and some vendettas demanded a price far higher than she had anticipated.

Across town, Jean-Luc's investigation took him into the labyrinth of Paris's underground tunnels; narrow, damp corridors forgotten by most and used only by those seeking anonymity. The walls held echoes of centuries past, whispering stories of power, betrayal, and bloodshed; a history he had studied diligently. His crew's flashlights flickered as they navigated through narrow passages beneath the Louvre, every creak and drip adding to the mounting tension. He paused, listening intently, sensing that they were approaching not just hidden chambers but the very nerve center of the killer's twisted saga. Somewhere in these depths, the final act lay in wait; an encounter that would demand everything he had brought to this dark pursuit, knowing that one wrong step could turn these shadows into his grave.

The truth was always more cruel than imagined. As Grace's story unfolded, her mind spiraled into fears rooted in her family's darkest secret; a legacy of corruption and shame wrapped around her brother's disappearance. Her pulse pounded louder with each passing second, the photograph trembling in her grasp. She knew the history wasn't just her own; it belonged to a bigger story, one woven into the roots of the town itself. Somewhere in her trembling hands was a piece of a puzzle now begging to be solved, even if it meant unearthing truths that would tear her apart. Her resolve was tested as her phone lit up again, revealing another message; this one explicit, threatening her to lay the photograph down and forget what she'd seen. But she couldn't turn away; not yet.

Meanwhile, Dubois's team uncovered a series of clandestine passages beneath the city, revealing a hidden network that seemed to stretch back through generations. Each tunnel seemed to breathe with the weight of past sins; the secrets kept beneath the very foundations of Paris. The killer was orchestrating a game of shadows, sending clues that connected the murders with ancient grievances and personal betrayals. Every step brought Dubois closer to a revelation that would shatter his assumptions; for the killer had been playing him all along, hiding behind layers of lies and misdirection. The lines between right and wrong blurred as the true face of vengeance revealed itself, dark and uncompromising. As he descended deeper into the gloom, Dubois understood that crossing this threshold meant risking everything; his safety, his sanity, and the fragile sense of justice he'd clung to for so long.

In the midst of chaos, Grace's decision hardened. She couldn't allow the darkness of her family's history to drown her, yet every step toward uncovering her brother's fate pulled her deeper into it. Her vision blurred with tears, but her resolve remained unbroken. She realized that her quest for truth was no longer just about revealing the past but about facing the consequences of vengeance itself. What she would find could destroy her entire world or set her free, but there would be no turning back now. The weight of her discovery pressed heavily, and with trembling hands she prepared to confront the ghostly remnants of her family's sins, knowing that the price of truth often meant paying in more than just memory. Somewhere in Paris, Dubois felt it too; that ominous shift in the air; as if history's most brutal secrets were ready to be unleashed, forever changing everything they believed in.

Chapter 25

The Closed Case, The Open Wound

The quiet suburban street seemed undisturbed as dawn broke over the neatly lined houses. Jeremy Collins sipped his coffee slowly, his gaze slipping past the freshly mowed lawns toward the curb where he'd found the photograph earlier that morning. It was a simple shot, black and white, capturing an old man in a weathered hat standing beside what looked like a crumbling stone wall. No big deal, he told himself; yet something about it pricked at the back of his mind. Suburbia's always been good at hiding darkness beneath its veneer of normalcy. That's what made this, he thought, slightly out of place; just enough to trouble him for no real reason.

He had no doubt that the photograph was insignificant, maybe just left behind by someone passing through. Still, he found himself staring at it for long moments, feeling an uncomfortable tug in his gut. Jeremy had grown up here, raised his kids here, yet the faint shadows of past scandals and unspoken grievances lingered beneath every smile and Saturday barbecue. The town's calm exterior hid a history more fractured than most of its residents wanted to admit. He'd brushed off the curiosity he felt, but that restless feeling refused to fade. Beneath the surface, something was waiting to surface; something that had nothing to do with a forgotten photograph.

Across town, in an aging apartment filled with stacks of unopened files and half-empty coffee cups, Detective Sara Ortega moved swiftly through digital archives, searching for clues connected to similar photographs from decades ago. Her sharp eyes flicked over names, dates, and locations, piecing together whispers of old land disputes, people disappearing without explanation, and whispers of corrupt deals buried deep beneath city hall records. These all seemed disconnected at first glance, yet she knew better. The dots were there, somewhere, waiting for someone brave enough to connect them. Her instincts told her this wasn't just about dusty history; something dark and unresolved had resurfaced, and it had a new face, a new weapon, now wielded by somebody willing to go to lethal lengths.

Back at the local library, Mark Evans, the town's historian, thumbed through yellowed newspaper clippings, eyes scanning for any mention of that strange photograph. His hands trembled slightly, disturbed by the memory of what he'd uncovered in an obscure ledger; an old land deed linked to a family long thought extinct, the same family involved in suppression and betrayal during the mid-twentieth century. Something about that ledger felt ominously familiar, yet unplaceable. As he read, he felt a sudden chill, as if an unseen presence was watching him. The history he uncovered had become more than just dusty paper; it now seemed intertwined with the current disappearances, with the killer's twisted obsession, with the shadow that refused to die quietly. Somewhere, beneath the layers of lies, a wound remained unhealed.

Michael Donovan, the local reporter with a reputation for digging into uncomfortable truths, prowled his modest office, scrutinizing a series of cryptic messages sent late last night. Each one contained fragments of coded language, references to old betrayals, and veiled threats. He'd been chasing leads for weeks; clues that pointed directly at powerful figures, hidden alliances, and a cover-up that went back decades. The killer's messages echoed with the same tone as those ancient secrets, a deliberate attempt to remind him that some truths refused to stay buried. Michael felt the fear coiling inward, cold and quiet, knowing that revealing the conspiracy could cost him everything, including his life. Yet, the lure of exposing the truth was stronger than ever. Something long-standing had fractured, and now, it threatened to swallow everything whole, splintering the fragile calm of the town forever.

The sun finally rose higher, casting harsh light on scenes of ordinary life that belied the chaos lurking just beneath. A wind stirred the trees, whispering secrets that no one seemed to hear. Shadows flickered in corners, unnoticed but always present. The past, uncomfortable and unquiet, was seeping into the present with unrelenting force. Jeremy clutched the photograph tightly, suspecting it was just a piece of a larger puzzle. Sara's relentless digital probing hinted at a vast network of deception; Mark's archival searches uncovered layers of betrayal rooted deep in history; Michael's messages signaled that someone was watching, waiting for the right moment to strike. As night threatened to return, so did the unsettling feeling; they'd only scratched the surface. The wounds of the past, once thought closed, were bleeding anew, and no one knew when or where they'd reopen; or what the full damage might be.

Also by Hamon de Quillan

Fiction:
- The Inner Circle.
- The Shadow Broker.
- The Last Train to Paris.

Non-Fiction:
- William Faulkner: A Life In Literature.